L. D. KNORR

The

Leviticus Mission

The RV Mysteries
Book ONE

The Leviticus Mission

FIRST SUNBURY PRESS EDITION
Printed in the United States of America
October 2011

ISBN 978-1-934597-54-5

Published by:
Sunbury Press
Camp Hill, PA
www.sunburypress.com

Camp Hill, Pennsylvania   USA

Acknowledgments

Thank you to my editor Jennifer Melendrez who corrected the thousand and one punctuation errors and whose suggestions made it a far better book.

Thanks to my wife Emily for making vital suggestions for the book and for tolerating my full-time retired presence while I commandeered a corner of our living room for my portable writing desk.

Thank you Sunbury Press for publishing my work.

And last but not least, a salute to all the millions of RVers across the country seeking adventure. I wish you smooth highways and level campsites.

****

Look for the next Hank and Helen Moran RV adventure. Book two of the RV Mysteries is in progress and will be published in the spring of 2012.

PART ONE

Chapter 1

Sunday, July 4th, 2010

Late afternoon was hot and muggy on the holiday weekend on Santa Rosa Island. The bath house at the public access to Pensacola Beach was rumored to be a place where the occasional degenerate might get lucky and meet the occasional like-minded degenerate for the purpose of doing what like-minded degenerates like to do.

The slim six foot tall man with dark hair was dressed in casual attire. Being a hot muggy day you would think he would be dressed in shorts and t-shirt instead of long black pants and white dress shirt.

He was noticed immediately upon entering the bath house by a man in blue swim pants sitting in the back corner. The man was pretending to be changing clothes after a hot afternoon on the beach. He watched the new arrival with interest as he stepped up to the urinal and proceeded to relieve himself with a contented sigh.

The man in the corner spoke, "Too hot to be going out on the beach dressed like that."

Zipping up and stepping away from the urinal and glancing back to the corner he answered, "Don't intend to go on the beach. I was just passing by and needed to make a pit stop."

"Well hell, guess that's allowed", was the reply from the corner.

"Who are you the bath house police?"

"No man, just making friendly conversation."

The man in the white shirt asked, "Didn't your mother ever tell you not to talk to strangers?"

"She did. Long time ago. But I never listened to her. Sorry if I bothered you, like I said, I'm just trying to be friendly."

The new arrival thought, *This would be the perfect time to start my mission. God must be presenting me with this opportunity.* He said to the man in the corner, "What's your definition of friendly? Just how friendly do you want to get?"

Corner man answered, "Now that depends on you. I'm known to get real friendly if you know what I mean. By the way my name's Jesse, but my friends call me Skeeter".

The new arrival thought to himself, *Why are all the little wiry guys called Skeeter? Probably for the same reason all big guys are named Bubba. Whatever that reason is?*

"Well, Skeeter, I'm Frank and my friends call me Frank", he said with a grin and added, "I think I do understand what you mean about getting friendly. Tell you what, I'm staying back at the Hampton. How about meeting me in the lounge at about seven thirty and we can have a nice friendly discussion about life."

"Sounds good to me, I think I can make it. Yeah, OK, I'll be there Frank", was Skeeter's excited reply. Skeeter thought his vigilance had finally paid off.

****

Frank was sitting in a booth and enjoying a Dewars on ice when Skeeter walked in. He motioned for Skeeter to join him in the booth.

"Have a seat", Frank said. "What will you have?"

Skeeter slid into the booth opposite Frank, "I worked up an awful beer thirst out on the beach today."

"You mean you were actually on the beach? I thought you just hung around in the bath house."

Extending his arms and turning them over Skeeter rebuked, "Don't get a tan like this sitting around in no bath house."

A dark haired waitress with a nametag that said "Beth" came by and Skeeter ordered a bottle of Corona. "No mug. Just bring the bottle. And hurry."

The compliant waitress was back thirty seconds later with the Corona and Skeeter chugged half of it before he came up for air.

"Better bring another one Miss Beth, this one won't last too long."

The waitress smiled and dutifully set out for another bottle of Corona.

The sun had gone down by the time they had a few rounds and Frank said he felt like going for a short ride.

"I was hoping we were going to, you know, get together up in your room", Skeeter said.

"We can get to that later", Frank replied. "I need to check something out before it gets too late. Why don't you come along."

"I guess I don't have anything better to do," Skeeter replied.

Skeeter followed Frank out to the parking lot and into Frank's new black F-250 diesel pickup.

"Wow. Nice truck. I would have guessed you were a luxury car type of guy. Thought you'd be driving a Lexus or something."

"Skeeter this truck is worth more than a Lexus and look around. You don't think you're sitting in luxury?"

Skeeter recalled the diesel option and noted the tan leather seats and the myriad of options including the in-dash GPS; the sticker price must've been north of sixty grand.

They left the hotel parking lot and drove over the Bob Sikes Bridge into Gulf Breeze, a small, quiet town located on the west end of the Fairpoint Peninsula between Pensacola and Santa Rosa Beach, accessed by causeways both north and south. The main artery between Pensacola and the beach runs through the east side of Gulf Breeze presenting heavy seasonal traffic. Most people, excitedly anticipating the beach, are unaware they are passing through a small town. The UFO incident of 1987 put Gulf Breeze on the map for a short period. A local man produced high quality pictures of UFO's that spread rapidly throughout the world's newspapers and magazines. The pictures were later proven to be a hoax.

Turning left onto Fairpoint Drive, Skeeter asked where they were going and Frank said he had to check something out near the point. After about a mile and a half Frank slowed the truck and turned into the Forest Lawn Cemetery.

Feeling a bit uneasy Skeeter uttered, "What are we doing here? Graveyards give me the creeps."

Frank said, "Take it easy, Skeeter. We won't be here long."

Frank proceeded down the narrow drive then made a three point turnaround at the second cross drive and parked facing back the way they entered. The cemetery was small but secluded with many full grown moss covered oak trees and dense shrubbery between sections of graves.

Frank got out of the truck and told Skeeter to get out; that he wanted to take a short walk. He needed to pay his last respects to a recently deceased friend. Skeeter hesitatingly obeyed trying to overcome his phobia of cemeteries.

Frank reached into the truck and removed a small .38 revolver from the console, and without Skeeter noticing, stuck it in his back belt. They walked a short distance and Frank told Skeeter to stop between two grave markers surrounded by shrubbery.

"Is this where your friend is buried?" Skeeter asked.

"I think it's somewhere around here," Frank said.

Frank pretended to be searching for the grave marker for his friend.

Skeeter asked, "What was your friend's name? I can help you look."

"His last name was Bixler. They said it was one of those small markers that just lay on the ground. Not a large upright headstone."

"That's gonna be hard to find. It's starting to get pretty dark."

"I think that's it right over there," Frank pointed in the direction of a grave surrounded by shrubbery on three sides. "Why don't you check the name, Skeeter. I'd do it but I have a painful knee."

Skeeter had to get down on hands and knees to read the inscription on the small marker. He started to say it was the wrong grave when three quick shots rang out. Frank said under his breath, "I think it was the right grave, Skeeter. Another pestilence removed from God's good earth. Fitting name, 'Skeeter.'"

Frank pulled Skeeter's pants down over his butt. "Good Lord," Frank thought, "he didn't even have underwear on." Frank reached into his shirt pocket and found the yellow post it note pad. He wrote a brief note and stuck it to Skeeter's rear end. He made sure he left nothing behind and calmly walked to his truck. He made his way back to Fairpoint Drive and took a left across the Pensacola Bay Bridge into Pensacola.

On the northwest side of Pensacola he slowly pulled into the Mighty Oaks RV Park located just off Interstate 10. It was past ten o'clock and was now the quiet time in the park. He quietly made his way back the gravel drive to his travel trailer, locked his truck, and entered his RV. Feeling thirsty he selected a bottle of water from the refrigerator and settled down into his rocker with his bible. He opened the bible to the third book of the Old Testament and smiled. He felt content in knowing his God would be pleased with him.

Chapter 2

Sunday, July 4th, 2010

The Gulf Breeze police department received a call from a woman at approximately 9:45 in the evening reporting that she just heard gunshots in the Forest Lawn cemetery. A patrol car was dispatched and made the short drive to the cemetery.

The officer drove slowly through the cemetery shining his flashlight from side to side but saw nothing out of the ordinary. He reported back to the station that all seemed normal. It was written off as teens probably setting off Fourth of July fire crackers as gunshots had not been heard in the peaceful town for years.

Monday morning, July 5th, 2010

The two Hartley brothers and three other boys were playing army in the cemetery taking cover behind the tomb stones to lie in wait for the approaching enemy.

Jimmy Hartley was crawling on his belly through the shrubbery for better cover when his fellow soldiers heard him exclaim, "Holy shit guys come here quick! There's a dead body over here!"

They all ran around the shrubbery to where Jimmy was and saw that he wasn't playing. Jimmy said, "I live the closest. We better go tell my mom." All five immediately ran back to the Hartley house and excitedly tried to tell Mrs. Hartley that they found a body in the cemetery. She amusingly told them there are lots of bodies in the cemetery. Jimmy replied, "But Mom! This one's on top of the ground and there's lots of blood and his pants are down and he has something stuck to his butt!"

Mrs. Hartley finally realized that the boys were serious and followed them back into the cemetery. Sure enough there was the body just as they described. She sternly told all the boys go back to her house and wait for her. They reluctantly obeyed and when they turned to head home she pulled out her cell phone and dialed 911.

Detective Ken LaFollette and his partner, Jack Barnes, were first on the scene. They arrived within ten minutes after the 911 call as the police station was only a mile away on Fairpoint Drive. Detective LaFollete asked Mrs. Hartley if she was the one who made the call.

"Yes I am", she replied.

"How did you find the body?"

"I didn't find it. My two boys and some other kids were playing army out here and they found it. They ran back to our house and informed me and I followed them here."

"Where are the boys now, Mrs. Hartley?

"I sent them back to the house to wait for me."

"Did they say if they touched anything?" Lafollette asked.

"I don't think so. They were pretty scared."

"OK, Mrs. Hartley, you are free to go. Give me your address and phone number. I'll want to stop by a little later to talk with the boys."

After she left, Ken turned to Jack and asked him what he thought.

"Well, Ken, it looks like a number of shots to the back of the head, almost execution style. Hard to tell who it might be with all the blood and all. Don't recall anything ever like this in all my years here in Gulf Breeze."

Jack was right. The only recent untimely deaths in Gulf Breeze had been suicides. In one a guy shot himself on his front lawn, and the other was a married couples' decision to end it all by murder/suicide. This definitely wasn't a suicide.

Ken said, "What's the meaning of the post it note stuck to his rear end? It looks like a bible verse, Lev 20:13."

Jack occasionally taught Sunday school classes at the First Baptist. "It's from the book of Leviticus. I think it's on the order of an anti-homosexuality passage about men who sleep with men and that they should be put to death, but not in those exact words."

Ken said, "Hmm, I'll call Sally later at the station. She always has a bible in her desk. In the mean time we have to get the coroner out here to examine and move the body. Can't even start to identify him in the position he's in. There's a wallet in his back pocket but I don't want to disturb anything until he gets here."

They searched for shell casings but found none. No distinguishable footprints were visible.

The Santa Rosa County coroner arrived fifteen minutes later along with another patrol car. Lafollette told the arriving officers to block off the entrance to the cemetery to keep the rubberneckers away.

The coroner pronounced the victim dead, took a few photographs, and said it was OK to move the body. Definitely not as dramatic as CSI Miami procedures.

Lafollette removed the victim's wallet, found his driver's license, and said, "Well hello Mr. Jesse Lutz."

Jack said, "Jesse Lutz, name sounds familiar. Yes! I think he was picked up last week out on the island on a vagrancy charge in the beach bath house. I remember my buddy from the sheriff's department talking about it. The guy was a real fruitcake. Tried to proposition some guy who didn't appreciate it and the guy reported it."

****

The officer who responded to the gunshot report the night before was one of the department's part-timers that beefed up the force during the summer months to help control the traffic out to the beach. The cursory drive through by the part-timer and the body concealment by the shrubbery were the reasons the victim was not found on the night of the murder.

****

The coroner's report on Jesse Lutz was finished in two days. The report revealed that the cause of death was three .38 caliber bullets to the back of the head. No anal penetration or semen were found on the victim. Apparently the shooter was not into homosexual acts. Only murder. Subsequent investigation went nowhere. No witnesses and no leads.

Chapter 3

Wednesday, July 7th, 2010

Homicide detective Hank Moran and his longtime partner, Gerry Baker, were lugging the last boxes of possessions from Hanks desk and locker out to his SUV. After thirty-two years with the Kenner, Louisiana police force he was finally calling it quits. After fourteen years as a patrolman and eighteen years as a homicide detective he decided it was time to take a break. The sixty-year-old detective needed some time off from the stress of daily confronting the dregs of society. He and his wife, Helen, had planned to do some traveling for a few months. After that he thought he might try out the life of a private detective.

His thirty-two years of duty were untainted. Sometimes the offers of graft were hard to resist, but he managed to stay clean. During his career he was awarded two officer of the year citations and one for detective of the year. He earned the detective of the year award for his aid to the N.O.P.D. in the aftermath of hurricane Katrina.

With the SUV loaded he turned to Gerry and said, "Well, this is it partner." There was a manly embrace then Gerry said, "Hank, let's get the hell back inside before I get emotional." Hank and his partner shared ten years of service together. Some good times and some bad times.

Five years ago Gerry was knocking on the apartment door belonging to the girlfriend of a suspected bank robber when a .45 caliber slug tore through the door and lodged in his chest narrowly missing his heart. To this day Gerry claims he never heard the report of the gun.

Hank followed Gerry back inside the station to say his goodbyes. It took him longer than expected as he must have received a hundred handshakes and good wishes. His hand was sore from all the handshakes and who knows what his wife Helen would accuse him of after smelling all the perfume left on his shirt from the hugs of the female officers and secretaries.

His last stop was at Captain Benson's office. Benson was the stocky, gruff commander of the Investigative Services Bureau. A position he held for the last eight years. Because of his appearance and manner he earned the nickname "N'anderthal" by his underlings.

Benson's door was always open. After hearing a knock on the door jamb Benson looked up and raised his bushy eyebrows when he saw Hank standing in the doorway.

"Permission to come aboard captain."

"Hell, Hank, I wish you *were* coming aboard instead of abandoning ship. We're going to miss you greatly around here. It will be hard to replace the detective with the continually highest closure rate in the department. I still don't know how you do it, but you have an uncanny knack for connecting the dots."

"I only deserve half the credit, Captain. You're forgetting I had a very good partner just as deserving as me."

"Hank, Gerry is going to need a new partner. I was thinking of teaming him up with Maxine Renault. With her recent promotion to detective she needs someone to show her the ropes. What do you think?"

"I think that would be a good move, Captain. I couldn't think of a better match for Gerry. He'd be very receptive to taking Maxine under his wing."

"I just wanted to see how you felt about that, Hank. If anyone should know Gerry it would be you. Well, when you get tired of lounging around the house or Helen finds you too much to live with twenty four hours a day give me a call. We'll always have a spot back here for you."

"I appreciate that, Captain," Hank replied. "Actually Helen and I will be living a whole lot closer together in the very near future. We're going to finalize our purchase of a motor home this afternoon. We plan to do some traveling for a few months this summer."

"Hank, I wish you would have let us throw a little retirement party for you but we all understand your wishes. We took up a nice collection and will be making a sizable donation to the policeman's fund in your name."

"Thanks, Captain. It's been a pleasure working for you, and who knows? Maybe someday I just might be knocking on your door jamb asking to come back. Well, I better get going. Helen is anxiously waiting."

"Hank, good luck in your new life and safe trips in your new motor home. Make sure to drop by and visit once in a while and send some postcards from far off places."

"I'll do my best, Captain"

"You always did, Hank. Now get the hell out of here and enjoy yourself. If anybody deserves it, you do."

With a final handshake Hank left the station.

Helen was waiting on the front porch when Hank pulled up in front of the house. She was two years younger than Hank and still a bundle of enthusiastic energy. She got into the passenger side of the SUV and excitedly said, "Let's go we're late. They're waiting for us at the dealer."

"Can't I even take a leak first?" Hank asked.

"You can go at the dealer's, let's go."

Luckily the RV dealership was only ten minutes away. They zipped into the lot at Lakeside RV Sales and Service and Hank immediately headed for the men's room. When he came back out Helen was already taking an inspection tour of the Fleetwood Bounder motor home.

After surfing the Web the last few months they settled on either a Winnebago Adventurer or a Fleetwood Bounder. Both of the floor plans they liked had dual commodes which was one of Helens top priorities. She always accused Hank of sitting too long. Actually she thought the extra half bath would be needed when their nine-year-old grandson, Chip, traveled with them.

On previous visits to Lakeside they took both models out for test drives. It was a hard decision but they finally decided on the Bounder as it cost thirty-five thousand less than the Adventurer. Hank reasoned that you could buy a lot of fuel for thirty-five grand. The full body black, gold, and tan paint job was kind of wild but Helen liked it. She said it looked like freedom in motion. Hank thought it looked like a five year old kid's scribble. More like chaos in motion.

The Bounder had a queen sized bed, nice sized shower, and an extra TV in the bedroom. The kitchen had a four door refrigerator with an icemaker. The cockpit had comfortable leather seats for the driver and passenger. Hank liked the built-in backup and side view cameras. The living area was complete with a dinette booth, leather sleeper sofa, and a euro recliner with ottoman.

They signed all of the paperwork for the financing and registration and Hank wrote out a sizable down payment check. The salesman shook their hands and told them the unit would be ready for pick-up the following afternoon. The motor home had to be detailed and a full checkout performed on all functions and equipment.

Thursday, July 8th, 2010

Hank and Helen followed the service tech around as he explained the operation of all of the Bounder's equipment and how to make the hookups at a campground. Hank questioned why the wastewater tank was labeled "BLACKWATER" instead of brownwater. The tech ventured a guess that blackwater sounds less yucky than brown as everyone could immediately visualize something disgusting if it was labeled brown. Hank suggested it must have been named by someone suffering with an intestinal problem at the time. Helen just rolled her eyes not appreciating Hank's try at humor.

They decided to tow Helen's Civic behind the Bounder for auxiliary transportation. When the Bounder was hooked up at a campground they could use the Honda for local sightseeing and runs to the grocery store. The service department had previously installed the tow bar hardware and the service tech instructed them on how to hitch up the "toad" to the Bounder. The Honda could be towed with all four wheels on the ground. He also gave them a few road tips on towing two of which were, "Take wide turns and DON'T EVER TRY TO BACK UP."

Hank and Helen decided it was futile to try to absorb all the information and instructions at one time. They would just have to learn by doing like most things in life. They stepped up into the motor home and after Hank had all the mirrors adjusted and found a comfortable driver's seat position, he confidently headed home with the Civic towed behind. Hank's one nagging thought was, *How the hell do you avoid backing up?*

Hank made it home safely and pulled into their driveway like he had been driving the big motor home all his life. They unhitched the Civic as half of it was left sticking out into the street. Helen backed it up and deftly pulled it into the parking space in front of the house.

"Well, that went well," Hank said. "Didn't have to back up yet. I'm ready to roll. How about we take a short shakedown cruise over to Biloxi to practice all the campground routines before we take off and become the wandering Morans."

Helen suggested that they might be able to hit a jackpot at one of the casinos to pay for the motor home. Hank told her not to worry about the finances as he had everything covered. "Let's just enjoy ourselves."

Chapter 4

Friday, July 9th, 2010

The short trip to Biloxi took only two hours even though Hank chose to take old Rt. 90. from Waveland for the last leg. They enjoyed cruising along the beach with the view of the Mississippi Sound. The Sound is a protected bay of the Gulf of Mexico and is the source of brown shrimp which is the mainstay of the regions seafood industry. The shrimp boats were busy on the horizon as well as the para-sailors and sea-doos closer to shore.

They located and checked into the Seaside Campground on Rt. 90 in Biloxi, circled around, and found their site. Hank unhitched the Civic and proceeded to back the Bounder into the campsite. The rear view camera with the in dash screen made it a breeze. He didn't even need any directional help from Helen.

Bill Anspach and his wife, Jenny, were lounging under the awning of their Winnebago motor home watching all the new arrivals. Hank had backed into his site next door and was extending his slideout when Bill jumped out of his chair and ran to Hank's rig and rapped loudly on the side of the slideout. Hank immediately let go of the slideout button and went outside to see what the noise was all about.

Bill said, "Hello, neighbor, I think you might be a bit too close to the electrical box to extend your slideout all the way." It had stopped an inch short of the box with six inches left to extend. The slideout is a feature that appeared in RVs over the last fifteen years. It is basically a room extension and makes a huge difference in the interior space of the RV. The increased space provided by slideouts was one of the main factors in the rise of full time RVers.

Hank said, "Damn, something else to add to the checklist. Thanks for your help. We're on our maiden voyage and have a lot of RV savvy to gain."

"No problem, neighbor. Stop over and sit a spell after you get set up."

After repositioning the Bounder, adjusting the level, hooking up the 50 amp electric cable, water and sewer lines, and the TV cable they were ready to relax. Hank was surprised that he completed all of the tasks within twenty minutes. He and Helen decided to accept Bill's invitation and go next door to formally introduce themselves to their new neighbors and to thank Bill once again for his help.

Helen and Jenny immediately hit it off like old friends. They discovered they both enjoyed playing the quarter slots and also both of their husbands had refused many times to set foot inside a casino.

Hank told them about his recent retirement from the Kenner police department and their decision to go RVing. Bill had retired about a year ago from his job as a news editor for the *Indianapolis Star*. They were touring the gulf coast from Apalachicola to Biloxi and then planned to head up to Chattanooga before going back to Indy.

Jenny wanted a tour of the new Bounder so she and Helen disappeared for a short time while their husbands were shooting the breeze. They returned a short time later and announced they were heading to the Grand to try out the slots for a while before making dinner.

After the wives left, Hank and Bill were enjoying some Icehouse longnecks when Bill noticed a rig pulling in three sites away. "What a damn coincidence. Here comes that crazy preacher we ran into back in Pensacola. What a weirdo. He has all kinds of bible verses on the sides of his fifth wheel, and to put it mildly he is kinda weird to talk to. He travels around holding tent revivals where he can find a sponsoring church. He says he only makes enough money to continue his mission of spreading God's will."

Hank took in the sight of the rig and Bill's summation of his run-in with the preacher. "Sounds like a worthy thing to do, Bill. Maybe he can do some good in the world even if he is a little weird. Actually lots of preachers are a little weird down here, or to put it better: over enthusiastic. After all this is part of the Bible Belt".

"You may be right, Hank, but out of curiosity Jenny and I attended his last revival over in Pensacola.

He's a real firebrand type preacher and rages on and on about sinners and how they will burn in Hell. One of his most vociferous rants is about homosexuals and how they are in the express lane for the Devil's inferno. He likes to quote a passage that I think he says is in the book of Leviticus where God proclaims that men who sleep with men will be put to death."

Hank spied a few bible verses while looking over the preacher's rig. "There is one from Leviticus right near the door. I think it says Leviticus 20:13." He went into the Bounder to retrieve Helen's King James Bible and came back and sat down again. It took him a few minutes to find the passage. "Yep, that's the one you were talking about. I'll read it to you . . ."

If a man also lie with mankind, as he lieth with a woman, both of them have committed an abomination: they shall surely be put to death. Their blood shall be upon them.

Bill sat shaking his head. "I hope no one in his audience takes him too literally."

Hank agreed. "I hate to tell you, Bill, but after spending over thirty years on a police force I know there are plenty of nuts out there crazy enough to follow through on something like that. At one time they put them in institutions but now they are out on the streets and sometimes living right next door."

With a smile Bill remarked that he hoped Hank didn't mean right next door at a campground. Hank laughingly assured him that present company was excluded.

A while later they spotted the preacher going around the campground passing out flyers. The preacher approached Bill's campsite and immediately recognized him. "Well, hello again. I believe we met back in Pensacola the other day."

Bill reached up and accepted the flyer the preacher handed him. "Yes, we did. Actually I went to your last revival. It was very informative and I must say entertaining."

The preacher replied, "The purpose of my revivals is to save people's souls. The program has to be entertaining to hold everyone's attention so I can direct them back onto a righteous path. Just remember the path to everlasting life is straight and narrow. Why don't you and your friend here come to my next meeting?" And with that the preacher moved on down the campground.

Hank asked to take a look at the flyer. "The revival is tonight at the First Baptist Church up in D'Iberville. His name is the Reverend Billy Brantley. The flyer has bible quotes around the edges. Here's that one again about putting gay guys to death."

Bill remarked that he hoped the preacher didn't think they were a gay couple. "He looked at us kind of funny when he called you my friend."

Hank jokingly replied, "Maybe we ought to start packing."

About two hours later Hank and Bill were laid back napping in their lounge chairs but woke up when Jenny and Helen returned from the casino.

Jenny remarked, "Bill, I think I just spotted that preacher we saw back in Pensacola."

"Yeah, you're right. We seem to be on the same righteous path. He passed by a while ago handing out flyers for another one of his tent revivals."

Jenny tried to stifle a yawn. "I think the only revival I need is a little something for supper and then a little nap before bedtime."

Hank noticed Helen was carrying a cup full of coins. "Looks like you had a little luck at the casino."

Helen shook the cup of quarters. "Yes, I did! I won about thirty bucks."

Hank thought a moment, smiled, and rubbed his chin. "Hmm, at that rate how long will it take you to pay off the Bounder?"

"You said you have that covered, smarty. I'll just add this to my mad money. Next time it will probably go right back into the slots anyways. I think I'm going to follow Jenny's suggestion about rustling up a little something for supper. Come on, Hank. Let's go over to our place. I'm anxious to try out my new kitchen."

18

The Morans thanked Bill again for his help and headed back to the Bounder. Reverend Brantley nodded as he strode by on the way back to his fifth wheel trailer.

****

Saturday, July 10th, 2010

Hank awoke early to the sound of reveille being played on a loudspeaker. He later found that the campground was located near the Keesler Air Force base. They played reveille every morning and retreat at the end of each duty day on the system they called "Giant Voice." He was amazed at how easily his mind placed him back in army boot camp forty-two years earlier as an 18-year-old recruit.

Helen wasn't awakened by the reveille call to rise as she was awakened much earlier by the 3 am train that sounded like it was barreling through the campground. She was now soundly back to sleep. Hank knew Helen would want him to locate the morning newspaper as she was a crossword puzzle junky. She enjoyed working the puzzles with her morning coffee. He found some quarters in her casino cup and headed out to the campground office.

On his way to the office Hank had to pass by the reverend's trailer. The reverend was just exiting his RV as Hank approached.

"Good morning, neighbor", the reverend said.

"Good morning, Reverend. Beautiful morning isn't it?" Hank replied.

"Yes, indeed" said the reverend. "A delightful day to do God's work".

Hank proceeded to the office and bought a paper out of the dispensing machine and headed back to the Bounder.

An hour later Helen was busy with the crossword puzzle and Hank was browsing through the rest of the *Sunherald*. Being a former homicide detective he naturally looked for articles on crime. A small item on the third page that was reported from the *Florida Sun* in Pensacola caught his eye.

Gulf Breeze detective Ken LaFollette reported that a witness has come forth in the July 4th brutal slaying of Mr. Jesse Lutz in the Forest Lawn cemetery. A waitress from the Hampton Hotel on Pensacola Beach stated she served drinks to Mr. Lutz and another gentleman on the night of the murder. When they left she went outside to smoke a cigarette and saw the two men drive out of the parking lot in a large black pickup truck. The man that accompanied Lutz is being sought for questioning. He was tall and dark haired and was dressed in dark slacks and a long sleeved white shirt. The Gulf Breeze police are still withholding details of the crime from the public but rumors persist that the murder was hate-related and involved a homosexual. It was also rumored that a note with a bible quote (Lev. 20:13) was fastened to the victim.

Hank immediately thought of what Bill said about attending Reverend Brantley's revival back in Pensacola. He saw that Bill was out puttering around his motor home and went next door to show him the article.

"Hey, Bill, what day did you and Jenny go to that preacher's revival?"

Bill turned around and thought a minute. "I think it was last Saturday evening."

"That was July third," Hank said handing Bill the newspaper. "Look at this article I found."

Bill read the article and scratched his head. "Do you think this has something to do with our preacher friend?"

"Well, look at the guy's description again and then look at the truck he uses to tow his fifth wheel trailer. I know they are only rumors about the hate crime and the bible quote, but in my experience rumors like this are usually true. Details always leak out."

"That may be true, Hank, but there are lots of black super duty trucks around. There's another one over in the next row just down from the preacher's."

"You may be right, Bill, I could be jumping to conclusions, but my gut tells me there is something to it."

"You sound like you are still on the job," Bill said. "This is the time in your life to relax now, Hank."

"I guess you're right, Bill. By the way, when are you and Jenny leaving for Chattanooga?"

"We'll be pulling out in the morning. We need to get each others' cell numbers in case we cross paths again," Bill replied.

"Will do. We'll see you in the morning before you pull out."

The Morans spent the day touring Beauvoir and the J.L. Scott Marine Education Center. Beauvoir was the retirement home of Jefferson Davis, the president of the Confederacy. Davis had spent his last twelve years at the home until he died of acute bronchitis and malaria while visiting New Orleans. The home was heavily damaged by hurricane Katrina but had since been restored.

The J.L. Scott Marine Education Center and Aquarium provides an educational experience of the diverse ecosystem and seafood industry that helped to shape Biloxi's history.

The reverend was sitting out reading the newspaper as they passed by on their return from sightseeing. Hank thought there was something different looking about the reverend but he just couldn't put his finger on it.

"Helen. I saw the preacher this morning when I went for your newspaper, and looking at him again just now there is something different about him. Did you notice anything?"

Helen thought a few seconds and said, "Maybe he just got a haircut."

"You may be right. His hair might have been a little longer this morning."

This seemed to satisfy Hank's curiosity and the habit to pay attention to details he had acquired by working over thirty years in a police department. He thought about what Bill had said about this being his time in life to relax.

At 5:00 there was a knock on the Bounder's door. Helen saw it was Bill from next door and let him in.

Bill said, "You folks have anything to eat yet?"

Helen said they hadn't and that they were going to go out to sample the local fare.

"Since this is our last night here, Jenny and I would like to invite you to go along with us. Some other campers were telling me about a place called Cajun Fried Chicken out on Pass Road in Gulfport. It's supposed to have the best fried chicken around."

"They are right," Helen replied. "A friend of mine and I ate there last year when we took a day trip over here to the casinos. My mouth is watering just recalling it. They once had two locations here on the Gulf Coast. The one on Highway 90 was wiped out by hurricane Katrina. The restaurant on Pass Road gets crowded so let's get there early. We'll be ready in five minutes."

Saturday evening, July 10th, 2010

The killer parked his truck and entered the Just Us gay bar on Division Street in Biloxi. Though he was not entirely familiar with the area he Googled gay bars in Biloxi and quickly found information on the Just Us establishment. Luckily the campground had free WI-FI.

The bar was not too crowded as it was still early for the regular Saturday night crowd. There were still enough early drinkers for him to accomplish his mission. He found a seat at the bar and ordered a bourbon over ice. He figured it wouldn't take long to be hit on as he tried to pass "I'm interested" glances around the room; he was right.

A guy dressed in a pastel blue shirt, Bermudas, and sandals unsteadily made his way to the bar and sat on the stool beside him. It didn't take a genius to tell he was already half in the bag. He introduced himself to the killer as Donny Fleet. The killer smiled and said his name was Mack Woods and bought Donny another drink. The bartender set a bottle of Corona in front of Donny and told him he better start slowing down or else he wouldn't make it through the rest of the night.

Mack thought, *Another Corona drinker.*

Donny told Mack he had just broken up with his partner of four years and was trying to drown his sorrows. Mack was willing to help him all he could.

The evening progressed, and Donny was cut off by the bartender. The bartender offered to call a cab for him. Mack said not to bother as he would drive him home.

Mack helped him outside and into his truck. Donny was still coherent enough to comment on the truck and said he was feeling a little sick and hoped he wouldn't throw up in it. Mack told to him to do it out the window if he had to as the outside could be washed.

Mack didn't have to worry though as Donny was asleep three blocks away from the bar.

Mack found the on ramp for the Interstate 110 spur and headed north.

He found route 15 north of Interstate 10 and proceeded north into the DeSoto National Forest. Fifteen miles north of Biloxi he pulled into a parking lot at one of the hiking trail heads. He parked with the passenger door side of the truck hidden from view from the road.

He opened the passenger side door and Donny, sleeping against the door, nearly fell out. Mack lowered him to the ground and quickly found the black plastic bag that he had stowed behind the seat and pulled it over Donny's head. He secured it by making an airtight seal around his neck with a few wraps of duct tape. The task was quickly accomplished before Donny even started to wake up.

Mack held him firmly down to the ground. There was little struggle as Donny tried a feeble last gasp of breath. He didn't want to leave the bag on his head for fear of fingerprints. Feeling no carotid pulse he sliced the tape with a box cutter and removed the bag. He marveled at the ease of accomplishing his mission. Nice and easy and quiet. Not like the one in Gulf Breeze.

He was so pleased with the events that he almost forgot to leave the calling card. He reached into the truck's center console and retrieved the post-it note and stuck it partially into Donny's shirt pocket.

Then he remembered part of the bible verse: *Their blood shall be upon them.* To fulfill God's command he took the box cutter and made a slice in the victim's cheek. Only a small amount of blood oozed out as the heart was no longer pumping. But it was enough to fulfill God's will.

He retraced the route back to Interstate 10 then headed to the campground. After quietly driving through the campground he locked the truck and entered his RV trailer, got a bottle of beer from the refrigerator, found a pack of peanut butter crackers, and settled into his sofa with the TV remote. He was content in believing he was an instrument of God and that God would be pleased with his deeds tonight.

Chapter 5

Sunday, July 11th, 2010

Bill and Jenny were making their final preparations for their departure when Hank and Helen knocked on the door. They exchanged cell phone numbers and email addresses and discussed future travel plans to see if their paths might cross again. Bill said they were heading to Chattanooga with a one night stopover near Birmingham. Bill wanted to see Rock City and Jenny wanted to ride the Inclined Railway. Then they were heading up to Bowling Green, Kentucky to tour the Corvette plant and The Corvette Museum. They planned to arrive home in Indianapolis in three weeks for their granddaughter's twelfth birthday.

Hank and Helen said they planned to leave on Monday to go back to Kenner to plan their future travels. They said so far the RV lifestyle was thoroughly enjoyable, especially meeting new people like Bill and Jenny. Hank told them to keep in touch and stated they will try to work a stopover in Indianapolis into their itinerary. Bill said they would leave the light on for them.

After a few hugs and handshakes the Anspachs went back to completing their final preparations for departure. After one final check that all loose items on the countertops were safely stowed, they pulled out of the campground about mid-morning.

Hank was sitting outside the Bounder and noticed that a few sites down Reverend Brantley was also preparing to leave. He already had his super-duty truck hooked up to his Montana fifth wheel trailer. After stowing the water hose, sewer hose, and electric cable he was also on his way. The reverend waved as he drove by.

Hank did a double take. *I must be going nuts. I swear the preacher's hair grew overnight,* he thought.

Hank went back into the Bounder and settled into the sofa to see if anything was on TV while Helen prepared a light brunch. They hadn't had time for breakfast with Bill and Jenny leaving. Hank was channel surfing when a news bulletin flashed on channel 13.

"A body was found at about eight o'clock this morning by some hikers arriving at a trail head on Route 15 in the Desoto National Forest. The Harrison County Sheriff's Department was handling the case. They stated it was an apparent homicide. The identity of the victim was withheld pending notification of next of kin. Further bulletins will be broadcast as details about the crime are received."

Helen talked Hank into taking the excursion boat out to Ship Island. The departure was at twelve noon from the Port of Gulfport. The hour long boat ride to the barrier island was a cool diversion from the humid day. They marveled at the leaping dolphins escorting the ferry. Someone on the other side of the boat said he spotted a large lemon shark. He claimed it was ten feet long. The lemon shark got its name from its yellow color.

The boat dock was at the end of a long boardwalk that led to the north side of the island. The sun and humidity was already brutal as they traversed the boardwalk and stopped for the brief tour of Fort Massachusetts.

The U.S. War Department started construction of the fort in 1859, but it was not completed before the start of the Civil War in 1861. Confederate forces occupied the fort in 1861 but soon abandoned it. Later in the year Union forces took over the fort. The fort was the staging area for the Union forces' successful capture of New Orleans in the spring of 1862. Later in the war it held Confederate prisoners. The fort was also the home of the 2nd Regiment of the Louisiana Native Guards. The African American regiment manned the fort during the last years of the war.

After the tour of the fort the sun baked them as they continued the boardwalk trek to the Gulf Beach side of the island. The ocean wave action was higher than on the protected beaches of the Mississippi Sound. Hank enjoyed wading in the crystal clear water and watched the small fish that swam around his feet, always on the lookout for something larger and more menacing. He didn't want to begin his retirement as part of the oceanic food chain.

The return ferries were scheduled for two-thirty and five o'clock. Helen asked, "Hank, how soon do you want to head back? I think I've had enough sun for one day."

"You are getting a little burned," Hank replied. Let's try to make the earlier boat."

After changing back into their street clothes in the bath houses they made it to the return ferry just in time.

****

Hank lowered the thermostat in their air conditioned motor home and tuned into the Channel 13 five o'clock news. They had additional information on the body found in the national forest. The victim's name was Donald Fleet and the cause of death was due to suffocation. The county medical examiner determined the time of death to be at approximately ten o'clock the previous evening. The Harrison County Sheriff stated they are following up on some leads in the case.

The news reporter then broke away to an interview of one of the three hikers that found the body. He stated they pulled into the parking lot just before eight o'clock in the morning. They immediately found the body upon exiting their vehicle. They thought it was someone sleeping at first but upon getting a closer look at the body they had no doubt the person was dead. They said the odd thing about it was the post-it note sticking out of the mans shirt pocket. They thought it read Lev 20:13, a bible verse.

Hank immediately sat up straight upon hearing the report. He said under his breath, "OK. This has gone way past the point of coincidence." He turned on his laptop and found the phone number of the Harrison County Sheriff's Department. Hank dialed the number and after explaining who he was and that he had possible helpful information on the homicide was put through to Deputy Reed.

"Hello, this is Deputy Reed. How can I help you?"

"Deputy Reed, this is Hank Moran. I am a recently retired homicide detective from over in Kenner and may have some useful information on last night's murder.

"Go on, Mr. Moran."

"Do you know about the murder in Gulf Breeze about a week ago? The victim also had a similar note fastened to his body. The crimes may be related."

"I personally haven't heard about the Gulf Breeze murder."

"There is a Reverend Brantley who just left the Seaside Campground who has the same bible verse on the side of his travel trailer and also on the flyers he passed out in the campground. I also found out from a fellow camper that the reverend was in Pensacola at the time of the Gulf Breeze murder."

"That's very interesting, Mr. Moran, thanks for the information. I'll make it a point to contact the Gulf Breeze authorities about the homicide over there and I will check into the Reverend Brantley. Give me your phone number in case I need to talk to you again."

Hank gave him his phone number even though he was sure the deputy already had it on caller I.D.

****

Sunday Evening, July 11, 2010

Jimmy Huxley, the bartender from Just Us, was at home and just finishing dinner when his phone rang. He hardly had time to say hello when an excited voice on the other end shouted in a half crying manner. "Jimmy! Did you hear what happened to Donny last night?"

"No, Dewayne. What happened?"

"It's all over the news," Dewayne said sobbing. "He was killed last night."

"Calm down, Dewayne. Tell me what happened!"

"The sheriff said he was murdered. Somebody killed Donny," Dewayne said with an uncontrollable sob. "It's all my fault. We had a fight two nights ago and I left him. If I had stayed he would still be alive."

"Dewayne, Donny was in the bar last night and was driven home by a stranger. It looks like he didn't make it home. I have to hang up right away to call the sheriff."

Huxley located the sheriff's number on the list of emergency numbers stuck magnetically to the refrigerator and dialed. After a short explanation for the call the dispatcher transferred him to the deputy in charge of the case.

"Hello, this is Deputy Reed. How can I help you?"

"My name is Jimmy Huxley and I am the bartender at the Just Us night club and I have some information about Donny Fleet."

"Please go on", Deputy Reed said.

Huxley continued, "Donny was drinking heavily in the bar last night because he had just broken up with his partner the night before. A stranger came in and sat at the bar and Donny decided to make a move on him. He normally wouldn't do something like that but he was already half drunk trying to forget about the breakup. The stranger said his name was Mack something. I couldn't hear all of their conversation cause I was busy tending bar. They had a few rounds of drinks and then I cut Donny off because he was getting quite loaded. I offered to call a cab to take him home but the guy named Mack said not to bother and that he would drive Donny home. Donny wanted to go with him and the guy hadn't had much to drink, so what could I do?"

Deputy Reed asked, "Can you give me a description of the guy called Mack?"

"He was about six feet tall, slender, and had dark hair, and had on dark pants and a white shirt," Huxley offered. "He also had an air about him like he was a professional person or something. I just had the feeling he wasn't gay. He just wasn't the type to normally patronize the bar, if you know what I mean."

"Did you see what kind of vehicle they left in?"

"No I didn't. By that time I was quite busy at the bar and didn't think to look."

"Mr. Huxley, I need you to stop in at the sheriff's office at ten in the morning. I am going to call in an artist to sit with you and make a sketch of the guy called Mack. In the meantime, call me immediately if you remember anything else that will help."

"I sure will deputy, and I will be there in the morning."

"Thank you again Mr. Huxley. You have been a great help. See you in the morning."

Earlier that evening Hank decided to question some of the other campers to find out if they knew where Reverend Brantley was headed to. He knew he shouldn't be doing the sheriff's work, but just being a week into retirement it was still too early to break the habit. He thought that with all the campers coming and going every day that he better get the information now before it was too late.

He decided to start with the campers next to the reverend's empty site. Hank introduced himself to the couple and asked them if they had talked to the reverend next door. They said they hadn't but that the couple across the drive in the maroon and black Tiffin had spent some time talking with him. Hank thanked them and walked across the drive to the Tiffin motor home.

He introduced himself to the lady who answered the door. Hank assumed the man looking over her shoulder was her husband. Hank told them he was trying to find out if the reverend mentioned where his next stop was.

She said, "Why yes, he was headed to Tennessee to a church just north of Chattanooga . . . I think he mentioned the town of Cleveland."

"Did you notice what time the reverend left the campground last night?"

"I am sure he didn't leave at all. He held a bible study and prayer meeting in the pavilion last night until about nine-thirty and then he walked with us back here to our motor home. Then the reverend said he was tired and went across to his trailer to turn in for the night."

Hank asked again "Are you positive he didn't leave the campground?

The man standing behind the woman spoke up, "I'm sure he didn't leave because I took our Pekapoo out for her evening walk after ten and the reverend's truck was parked by his trailer. He still had some lights on in his trailer and I noticed the reverend moving about inside."

Hank thanked them for the information and walked back to his Bounder scratching his head. He thought that maybe he had the good reverend pegged wrong after all

since he was still here in the campground near the time of
the murder.

Hank called the Harrison County Sheriff's Department
and asked the dispatcher for Deputy Reed. The dispatcher
told Hank that the deputy was gone for the day. Hank
requested that they contact Deputy Reed and have him call
Hank Moran as soon as possible. He added that the deputy
has his number.

Five minutes later the deputy called back.

"Good evening, Mr. Moran, or should I still address you
as Detective Moran?"

"Good evening, Deputy Reed. I am still trying to shake
out of the detective mode so either one will do. Sorry to
bother you this late but I have additional information on
the Reverend Brantley I told you about earlier this
evening."

"It's no bother, Mr. Moran. What do you have?"

"Well, Deputy, I may have been wrong about the
reverend. I found out from a fellow camper that the
reverend held a bible study and prayer meeting here at the
campground last night and didn't leave the grounds at all
around the time of the murder."

"Thanks for the additional information, Mr. Moran. Now
I won't have to waste my time pursuing the reverend."

"Is any progress being made on the case?"

"We are making progress. In fact a witness came
forward that may have eyeballed the killer. We hope to
publish an artist's sketch on the evening news tomorrow. A
bartender at a gay bar in D'Iberville served drinks to the
victim and the suspected killer and saw them leave
together. I really shouldn't be telling you this so keep it
confidential. I did make a check on you with the Kenner
Police Department and they hold you in very high regard."

"Deputy Reed, could I ask you a favor? I am leaving in
the morning to go back to Kenner but I would like to see
the sketch in case it looks like anyone I've seen around the
campground. I still have a feeling that this all ties in
somehow with the reverend. Would you please email the
pic to me since it will become public knowledge?"

"I think I can do that as a professional courtesy, but I'll have to have the sheriff OK it first. Give me your email address."

Hank gave him his email address, thanked the deputy, and wished him good luck in solving the murder. The deputy thanked him once again for his help and ended the call.

Chapter 6

Monday Morning, July 12th , 2010

While Hank was starting to prepare the Bounder for the
short trip home to Kenner he remembered that Bill and
Jenny were on their way to Chattanooga. Possibly on the
same route as the preacher. He was sure that Bill had not
heard about the murder here in Mississippi as they had
departed before the news bulletin appeared on TV. He
dialed Bill's number and the call was answered on the
fourth ring.

"Hello. Bill Anspach here."

"Bill. This is Hank. I just wanted to fill you in on what
happened down here after you left yesterday. I assume you
are on your way to Chattanooga?"

"Yes we are. We just left the campground in Alabaster,
Alabama and we're heading up Interstate 459. What
happened down there?"

"There's been another murder here, Bill. It happened on
Saturday night and was reported on the news late Sunday
morning. And guess what, the same bible verse note was
left on the victim."

"I assume the victim was also gay?" Bill questioningly
replied.

"I don't know for certain yet, but the victim was picked
up in a gay bar in D'Iberville. I talked with the deputy
handling the case and he promised to email an artist's
sketch of the suspected killer."

"They have a suspect?"

"Yeah, the bartender remembered the victim leaving
with someone the night of the murder."

"Do you think the preacher is involved in this one?"

"I suspected him at first, Bill, but I checked around the
campground and it seems the preacher was holding a
prayer meeting here at the campground at nearly the same
time and has a good alibi. I also found out he is heading to

33

a church just north of Chattanooga. Keep an eye out for him."

"What is this with me and the preacher being on the same righteous path?" Bill replied.

Hank said he would call him if he had any further news and wished them a safe trip and to let them know when they will make it back to Indianapolis. Bill said he would call them when he has a firm date.

Hank and Helen made it back to their home in Kenner right after noon time. They busied themselves doing a little cleanup of the motor home and then started to think of their itinerary for the next two months.

They were both Elvis fans and had to include a stop in Tupelo, Mississippi to see Elvis' birthplace and then to Graceland in Memphis. They eventually wanted to travel to the northern peninsula of Michigan, then across Canada to Montreal, down to Lake Champlain, Cooperstown, New York, Pennsylvania Amish country, the Blue Ridge Parkway in Virginia, and then home. They also had promised Bill and Jenny they would stop in to visit them in Indianapolis.

They decided it would be a nightmare to try to make all the advanced campground reservations for the entire trip as they didn't want the stress of being held to a rigid time frame. If the campgrounds near where they wanted to stop didn't have a site, they could always dry camp. The Bounder was equipped with a generator and large holding tanks to keep it comfortable for a day or two. RVs were always welcome to spend the night at most Walmart parking lots, but Hank said they would only stop there as a last resort.

Helen suggested that once they were on the road and knew where they were headed they could make reservations a few days ahead of time. Hank agreed to Helen's always present logic. It seemed like a good plan to him.

Hank was in the process of making online reservations in Tupelo when his computer chimed to let him know that he had just received an email. He interrupted the Tupelo reservation and clicked on his email icon.

He saw that it was from the Harrison County Sheriff's Department. It was from Deputy Reed who wrote that the artist's sketch of the main suspect in the murder of Donald Fleet was attached. Hank clicked on the attachment and the sketch appeared in a few seconds.

Hank stared, transfixed at the picture for a short time and then called for Helen to come take a look at something. Helen came into the spare bedroom that Hank used for his office and stood behind his chair. Hank told her to take a good look at the picture on his computer screen and tell him who she thought it looked like.

Helen bent slightly to look at the picture and said, "The face looks familiar. Is it someone we know?

"Think back to this past weekend at the Biloxi campground", Hank replied.

Helen looked a little closer at the picture and said, "I think it looks like that preacher that stayed a few sites down from ours."

"That's what I thought, too. I just wanted you to look at it for a second opinion."

Helen went back about her business and Hank clicked on the reply button of the email.

Deputy Reed,

Thanks for sending the sketch. This may sound a little crazy but the picture looks a lot like the Reverend Brantley I had talked to you about. I know I told you he had an alibi for the night of the murder but it sure looks like him in the sketch. I believe the preacher needs further looking into. If I can be of any further help please don't hesitate to contact me.

Thanks again,
Hank Moran

The two murders and the mystery about the good reverend were really starting to work on Hank. He knew he shouldn't get involved with the cases but being only a week into retirement as a homicide detective the urge was too strong to resist. He didn't know if the preacher was actually the killer but he was sure the crimes were somehow centered about him. He didn't want to imagine what Helen's reaction would be, but he knew he had to help track down the preacher.

Hank went into the kitchen and sat down at the table in the breakfast nook. Helen could tell he was bothered by something. "What is it, Hank? You've been fidgety ever since you got that email from that deputy."

"Helen, I know you might get upset but I want to get on the trail of the preacher and get to the bottom of the murders surrounding him.

"I kinda knew this was coming, Hank, and prepared myself for it. And really it might actually be a fun adventure to travel around the country and bring a serial killer to justice."

Hank almost fell out of his chair when he heard Helen's answer. "Helen you're a saint. Now I know why I married you."

"You're just finding out now why you married me?"

"Helen, I was thankful from day one that I married you. How you put up with being a policeman's wife all these years is beyond me. It takes a special kind of person for that. I just want to let you know how thankful I am for having you as my wife all these years."

"Hank, I've always admired how you handled your job with the utmost integrity and was proud to be your wife, and I still am. So now, sweetheart, let's go find us a preacher."

"Helen, you said those same words thirty years ago."

****

Monday Afternoon, July 12th

Hank accessed the internet and Googled churches in Cleveland, Tennessee. He found six good prospects and started calling the numbers listed for the churches. He had no luck with the first three churches. Fourth on the list was The Journey Church. A woman answered on the third ring. "Hello, Journey Church. Betty Stiles speaking."

"Hello, Ms. Stiles. This is Hank Moran from over in Kenner, Louisiana. I am trying to locate a Reverend Billy Brantley who specializes in tent revival meetings. I heard he was coming to your area and wondered if your church might be sponsoring him for a revival."

"Mr. Moran, you are in luck. Yes, we have Reverend Brantley scheduled for a tent revival on Thursday evening. My husband, the minister, is out making arrangements to rent a tent as we speak."

"I know the reverend travels around in a travel trailer. Do you happen to know which campground he is staying at?"

"No, I don't. Actually, I think he is not due here until tomorrow."

"Thank you for the information, Mrs. Stiles. My wife and I just might make it over there to see the reverend."

"All are welcome at our church. We would be delighted to have you and Mrs. Moran attend the revival."

"Thanks again and goodbye, Mrs. Stiles."

Hank called out from his office, "Helen. I located the preacher."

"Is he over in Cleveland, Tennessee?"

"Not at the moment, but he has a revival there on Thursday evening."

Helen appeared in the doorway. "Do you think we could make it over there by Thursday?

"It should be no problem if we leave tomorrow."

"How long do you think we'll be gone?"

"I think we should take enough clothes for at least ten days. We can take whatever food we have and do groceries along the way."

Helen thought for a minute. "We'll have to get online and stop the mail and the newspaper. Let's start hauling things out to the Bounder."

Hank said, "I'll make the campground reservations and be right with you."

Hank found an opening at the K&K campground near Prattville, Alabama and the KOA near Cleveland, Tennessee. He decided to call Bill to see if they had arrived in Chattanooga.

Hank was just about ready to hang up when Bill answered, "Hello, Hank. What's up?"

37

"Hello, Bill. Helen and I are leaving in the morning for Cleveland, Tennessee and should arrive there on Wednesday. I was hoping you and Jenny will still be in the area."

"We're just now setting up in the campground just off of the intersection of Interstates 24 and 75. We planned to do two days of sightseeing and leave on Thursday morning. We decided to stop in Nashville before heading up to Bowling Green."

"Hey, do you think we can get together Wednesday evening? We'll be staying at the KOA about twenty miles north of you."

"Hank, did you and Helen decide to become roving detectives and track down that preacher?"

"You guessed right, Bill. There's just too much going on there to be coincidence. And an old detective like me just can't let it pass. Helen said she's looking forward to the adventure."

"OK, Hank. I guess we'll see you on Wednesday.

"See you then, Bill."

In spite of all they had to do Hank and Helen managed to leave early Tuesday morning for the two day trip to Tennessee. Hank was quickly becoming adept at driving the big rig and maneuvering around gas pumps without needing to back up. He also managed to keep plenty of space for the slide outs when maneuvering into a site.

At the stopover in Prattville Helen enjoyed shopping in the western store at the K&K Campground. However, she was unable to talk Hank into buying a pair of western boots.

Hank inquired at the front desk if a Reverend Brantley happened to check in the previous Sunday. He made sure to note that he would have been driving a black F-250 pulling a Montana fifth wheel. The girl behind the counter checked the records and said no one by the name of Brantley had checked in on Sunday or Monday.

Wednesday, July 14th

Hank and Helen left Prattville early on Wednesday
morning as they were anxious to get up to Cleveland as
soon as possible. Two hours into the trip they reached a
section of Interstate 59 above Gadsden, Alabama that gave
their internal organs a tremendous shaking that Hank was
sure would cause premature aging. Each small section of
the concrete highway was buckled so that set up some
kind of harmonic wave action in the rig that wanted to tear
it apart. Helen noticed that all of the semi trucks were
traveling only in the passing lane. She assumed the road
was smoother over there and suggested Hank try it: She
was right. They stayed in the passing lane the rest of the
way to the Georgia state line. As soon as they crossed the
border it was smooth sailing. The Alabama Highway
Department had just slipped to a rating of two out of ten
in Hank's estimation. He made a mental note to take a
different route on the way home.

After stopping to eat lunch at the Tennessee Welcome
Center they arrived at the Cleveland, Tennessee KOA just
after two o'clock in the afternoon. Hank kept an eye out for
the preacher's rig as they slowly motored to their RV site.
They didn't spot it on the way in, and Helen suggested they
should take a walk around the campground after they were
finished setting up the Bounder.

Chapter 7

Wednesday, July 14, 2010 - Cleveland, Tennessee

Hank and Helen decided to take a walk through the campground to see if the preacher had chosen the KOA for his stay in Cleveland. They strolled through the upper section and were partway into the lower sites when Helen spotted a Black F-250. "Hank, is that the preacher's truck up ahead?"

"I'm not sure, let's get a closer look."

Upon approaching the trailer Hank realized it wasn't the preacher's rig.

"That's not his rig. He has a Montana fifth wheel and that one is a Denali. And besides there are no bible quotes on it. I don't think there are any other campgrounds close by. I wonder where he is staying."

"Do you still have the phone number of the church where the preacher is holding the revival?" Helen asked. "You could call the church and see if they know where he is."

"I have it programmed in my cell phone," Hank said as he was pushing the call button for the number.

"Journey Church, Betty Stiles speaking."

"Hello again, Mrs. Stiles. This is Hank Moran from over in Kenner, Louisiana. I talked to you a few days ago about the Reverend Brantley and you said he is having a revival there tomorrow night."

"Yes, I remember your call, Mr. Moran."

"Mrs. Moran and I are in the area and we are planning to attend the revival. I was wondering if you knew at which campground the reverend was staying."

"Actually Reverend Brantley is staying right here on the church grounds. We were able to provide him with a water hookup and electric service."

"Is he planning to leave on Friday morning?"

"I think he is. He said he has another revival up in the tri-cities area on Saturday evening."

"Well, business is sure looking up for the reverend. We'll see you at the revival tomorrow night, Mrs. Stiles.

"You and Mrs. Moran are surely welcome. See you then."

That evening Hank and Helen took the short drive down Interstate 75 to the Trav-L-Park campground to visit the Anspachs. They were happy to keep in touch with their newfound friends. They spotted their Winnebago and parked in the empty site next to it as Bill and Jenny waved to them from under the motor home's awning.

The Anspachs had a cold pitcher of margaritas ready and waiting. "Well, Hank, did you track down that preacher yet?" Bill said.

"As a matter of fact we did. He happens to be staying on the grounds of the Journey Church up in Cleveland. They have water and electric hookups for him. We plan to attend his tent revival tomorrow evening to keep an eye on him. Why don't you join us?"

"Thanks for the invitation, Hank, but one of Reverend Billy Brantley's revivals is enough for us. It's sort of like celebrating Mardi Gras on Bourbon Street: everyone should experience it once in their lifetime. Only once is needed. No need to go back."

"I know what you mean, Bill. We live in the area and went to Mardi Gras one time in forty years," Hank said with a chuckle.

"Hey, I just got an idea," Bill said. "I was talking to my old boss at the newspaper about our travels and he suggested I write a weekly article for the travel section. Sort of like 'On the Road with Bill and Jenny'. He thought it would be of interest to the readers since more and more people are getting into RVing. It would be about interesting places we visit and interesting people we meet. I just might write about you and Helen and your traveling detective adventures."

"I wouldn't be too hasty about writing about us just yet. So far we haven't done anything," Hank said.

"I guess I'll just have to wait for the big shootout then," Bill said.

"I sure hope it doesn't come to that," Helen said. "We're just snooping around right now out of curiosity."

"So, how did you enjoy the sights around Chattanooga?" Hank said changing the subject."

"We saw Rock City and took a ride up the Inclined Railway," Bill said. "It was just like most of the other tourist traps. Once you have seen them, no need to go back."

"You mean like Mardi Gras on Bourbon Street?" Hank asked smiling.

"You guessed it!"

"I hope you make it more interesting in your article," Helen said.

"Don't worry Helen, I have a gift for gab and I'll juice it up enough to keep it interesting."

"Well, maybe Nashville and the Opry will be more entertaining for you. Are you still planning to leave in the morning?"

"Yeah, we'll be pulling out about mid-morning".

Jenny had prepared a delicious snack of marinated barbecued shrimp that were marinated in olive oil, lemon juice, and Slap Ya Mama Cajun spices. The shrimp were bought fresh from the dock down in Biloxi and quickly frozen for their trip back home.

"These shrimp are out of this world", Helen said. "We're not leaving until I get the recipe."

Hank was too busy stuffing his face to comment one way or the other.

On the way back to the KOA in Cleveland Hank decided to take a drive by the church to check out the preacher. The Magellan GPS announced they reached their destination on the right, and Hank drove slowly past the church on Lee Highway. He spotted the reverend's fifth wheel on the far side of the church. A tent was already erected on the grass lot beyond the preacher's rig.

Hank slowed and made a u-turn and found a small parking lot where they had a view of the church grounds. "I don't see the preacher's truck. Looks like he's not at home."

"Do you think we should stick around awhile and see what time he comes home?" Helen asked.

"Good idea. That way we would have a timeline on the preacher in the event of another murder. It's ten-fifteen now. The two murders both took place right around ten. I think we should stick around until about eleven-thirty. That should give him enough time to get back home."

"This is exciting!" Helen exclaimed. "A real life stakeout. What do we do for entertainment?"

"We don't do anything. We just keep our eyes and ears open and watch."

Fifteen minutes later Hank smiled when he looked over at Helen who was sound asleep. "Well I guess the excitement was too much for her."

At 10:50 Hank saw the preacher's truck slow and enter the church's parking lot: he was alone. He parked, locked his truck, and entered the trailer. The trailer's interior lights stayed on for another fifteen minutes and then it went dark.

Hank woke Helen up when they reached their motor home at the KOA.

Earlier that evening

The killer entered the Images nightclub in Chattanooga right when happy hour was ending at 9:00. The techno music was throbbing out of the overhead speakers as a small crowd gyrated on the dance floor. He found a seat at the bar which had a view of the dance floor. When the bartender asked what he would have he ordered an Old Grandad over ice.

He stayed for two drinks and realized the evening was a bust. There was only a small crowd in the club that was made up of small groups of close friends. He left the nightclub realizing his chances of attracting his next victim were zero. Perhaps another night might prove more fruitful.

Chapter 8

Thursday evening, July 15, 2010, Cleveland, Tennessee

"What do you wear to a tent revival?" Helen asked.

"I don't think it really matters," Hank replied. "It won't be like going to Sunday church. I would guess people will arrive just as they are."

Helen opted to wear a pair of navy blue slacks and a long sleeved white blouse. She wasn't sure just how bad the mosquitoes would be or how cool it would get in the evening. Hank braved it with a pair of dress jeans and a short sleeved red and white Izod golf shirt.

The tent revival at the Journey Church was scheduled to run from seven to nine. Hank and Helen arrived fifteen minutes early to watch the arriving crowd. People were arriving in droves and it was apparent there would be standing room only for the event. Many people brought their own folding chairs in anticipation of a huge turnout. Hank had been correct that people were dressed mostly in casual clothes for a comfortable summer evening. Hank and Helen took their seats in the metal folding chairs near the back of the assemblage.

A Christian group was playing gospel music as Reverend Brantley made his appearance. He sat facing the congregation on a raised platform that appeared to be newly constructed for the occasion out of unpainted two bys. A small choir took their places near the back of the makeshift stage. Just as the program was ready to begin Hank noticed a black F-250 arrive and park near the back of the tent. The driver, who had a strong resemblance to the reverend, found a place to stand along the left side about even with the third row of seats. The reverend made eye contact with the late arrival and nodded seeming a little perplexed.

Reverend Stiles of the Journey Church, along with his wife, Betty, took the stage at the podium and welcomed the congregation to the Annual Journey Revival. He stated that after attending the evening's festivities anyone who felt the Calling was more than welcome to attend Sunday services at the church.

Reverend Stiles introduced Reverend Brantley and told the congregation that the reverend would be speaking to them in the second half of the program. Reverend Stiles would address the congregation first on the importance of living a Christian life in today's troubled times. Following Stiles' address the band was scheduled to entertain as donation plates were circulated among the crowd. Barbecues, sweet tea, and soft drinks were available for purchase from the churches ladies auxiliary concession.

Before Reverend Stiles' address, Reverend Brantley left the stage and returned to his travel trailer to put the finishing touches on his sermon. Hank noticed that Brantley returned a minute later with a folding chair for the driver of the F-250. He said a few words to the person and then returned to his trailer. Seeing them briefly side by side Hank realized that both of them resembled the police sketch of the Harrison County suspect. Helen agreed with his assessment. Helen also remarked that she thought the truck he arrived in was the same truck they spotted back at the KOA.

While Reverend Stiles was addressing the congregation, Hank went out the back of the tent to the F-250 and wrote down the tag number in the small spiral notepad he was never without. When he returned to his seat beside Helen he whispered to her that a KOA camper I.D. card was hanging from the rear view mirror of the truck. It was the same truck they spotted at the campground. Helen acknowledged the new information with a nod and a smile.

Reverend Stiles concluded his address with a prayer for the recent tornado victims in the area. He informed the audience that a portion of the revival's donations would be forwarded to affected needy families. He pleaded for everyone to give generously. Members of the church council moved among the congregation with collection plates as the Christian band played an up-tempo arrangement of "Faith of a Little Seed."

During the intermission that followed Hank and Helen enjoyed a barbecue and sweet tea from the ladies auxiliary booth. After twenty minutes of mingling the congregation was summoned to return to their seats for the remainder of the program.

After everyone was settled Reverend Brantley took the stage, stood at the podium, and paused, looking out over the expectant audience.

Finally he began in a loud excited voice, "God knows you! Yes, each and every one of you. He knows what you do. He knows what is in your heart. He knows if you are a faithful believer in His beloved son, Jesus, and He knows if you are a sinner destined to live eternity in the fiery realm of Satan's Hell. HE KNOWS YOU! And right now, before it is too late, YOU MUST GET TO KNOW HIM!"

Brantley continued his show becoming more animated with every word. The congregation's responses of amens and hallelujahs spurred him on even further. Hank and Helen, who had never attended a tent revival, sat and looked around in amazement at the fervor of the crowd.

Helen tapped Hank's arm and told him to look at the acquaintance of Brantley sitting at the end of the third row. The man was sitting there with his head back, eyes closed, and arms extended towards heaven. From Hank's vantage point he could see the man's lips continually moving in some sort of chant.

Brantley continued his presentation, and not to Hank's surprise, started his tirade against homosexuals quoting the book of Leviticus and other Old Testament passages. Once again Helen poked Hank's arm and motioned for him to look at Brantley's acquaintance. The man was now rocking back and forth and sometimes in a circular motion while continuing his chant. No one else in the congregation seemed to give a second thought to the man's actions as Brantley kept their rapt attention.

Brantley finally concluded his forty-five minute sermon to the amens, hallelujahs, cheers, and applause of the congregation. Hank thought Reverend Stiles would undoubtedly be pleased with next Sunday's turnout at Journey Church.

As Reverend Brantley left the stage he put his hand on the shoulder of his acquaintance, said a few words, and returned to his trailer.

Hank and Helen had a hard time deciding what to do next. Should they stake out the reverend's trailer or check back at the campground to see if Brantley's acquaintance headed home to his fifth wheel? Helen suggested they return to the campground to see if the man returned then they could drive back to the church to check on Brantley. Once again Hank conceded to Helen's logic.

When they returned to the campground they noticed that the man had not returned there. Hank thought the man should have had plenty of time to get back before they did as they saw him leave the revival about ten minutes ahead of them. Hank was also not the speediest of drivers. After refreshing themselves they got back in the Honda and returned to the Journey church.

Church members were in the process of cleaning up the area when they pulled into the lot. The reverend's truck was nowhere in sight. Hank said, "Well, partner, it looks like we lost track of them both. Why don't I drop you off back at the campground to watch for the mystery man and I'll come back here and watch for the reverend? We need to at least see what time they arrive home since we lost the opportunity to tail them."

Helen found a window in the Bounder from where she could observe the driveway leading to the mystery man's rig while Hank once again found a spot in the small parking lot across from the church.

Hank was just about ready to nod off at 11:30 when the reverend's truck slowed and turned into the church parking lot. Hank watched as the reverend entered his fifth wheel alone. Figuring the reverend was in for the night he headed back to the campground. A black F-250 entered the campground in front of him. It was the mystery man. Hank glanced at his watch. Time was 11:52.

Earlier that Evening

The killer once again entered the Images night club in Chattanooga. The timing was later than the night before and the crowd was large and boisterous. He managed to

47

find a seat at the bar and ordered another Old Granddad over ice. Glancing around the club he picked out at least five potential victims and smiled.

After his second drink he noticed one of the potential victims saying goodbye to his friends preparing to leave. The killer left his empty drink glass on the bar and strode out to the parking lot. He was waiting by his truck when the victim appeared.

He shouted, "Hey, fella, could you give me a hand? I have a drunk friend over here sitting on the ground and need help getting him into my truck. He's over here on the passenger side."

When the victim rounded the front of the truck he saw there was no one sitting on the ground. He turned to speak but was hit by a projectile that penetrated his right shoulder.

Two minutes later he was sitting in the passenger seat slumped against the doorjamb.

Friday morning, July 16th, Chattanooga

The employees of Ruby Falls were making their way into the mountainside parking lot to prepare for the onslaught of tourists. Ruby Falls is a 145 foot high water fall located within Lookout Mountain. Anyone traveling within one hundred miles of Chattanooga has seen the billboards beckoning, "SEE RUBY FALLS".

Becky Wilcox screamed as she exited her Hyundai at the far end of the lot. Lying just off the edge of the lot in front of her car door was the body of a man. The body was bare-chested with a large X carved into the flesh. Blood had coagulated in the wounds coloring the X a dark brownish red. The man's face appeared like he was sleeping. A large stone tucked under the man's chin weighed down a note placed in the V formed by the top half of the carved X.

The note read:

Lev 20:13
FIRE AND BRIMSTONE NEXT

PART TWO

Chapter 9

Mt. Dora, Florida - Fourteen Months Earlier

The members of the small church council sat dour-faced around the folding table used as a conference table. They were sitting on metal folding chairs awaiting the arrival of their minister.

Joe Teasdale, the newly elected council president spoke, "I just want to make certain that we are still unanimous in the decision to let the minister go. I know one or two of you like the way Reverend Brantley has been conducting the services, but our congregation is dwindling and we will not be able to keep the doors open at the present rate of contributions."

Teasdale passed out small strips of paper ballots that said only "yea" or "nay" with a check box beside each. "I wanted to keep this vote private with no recriminations. Please vote and return the ballots to me."

The small group quickly voted and passed the ballots to Teasdale. After the short time to tally the ballots he spoke, "The vote is five 'yea' and one 'nay.' Council, it looks like we are not unanimous, but we have our majority."

He no sooner finished speaking when the minister walked into the room. "Reverend Brantley, please have a seat," Teasdale said. He continued after the reverend was seated, "As you may know our congregation has been dwindling and the council has come to the decision to open our church to all who would like to come and worship with us. And by 'all' that even means members of our gay community will also be invited. We know only too well your position on the matter and we feel you are no longer the right person to conduct our ministry. Therefore, we are letting you go. I think it would be best to immediately remove all your personal belongings from the study and leave. I have a small check in the amount of three hundred dollars for your severance. With the present financial condition of the church we cannot give you more."

The reverend sat dumbfounded in his chair and slowly took in what the council president had just said. Then with his anger coming to a boil he bolted out of his chair and said, "You are all going to burn in Hell. You know you will be going against God's proclamations if you allow those abominations to worship with you. You have all been coerced by the Devil and all for the almighty dollar."

With that outburst, the reverend retrieved his few possessions from the study and stormed out of the church. He was no sooner out the door when he stormed back in and slammed the severance check down on the table in front of the council president. "Keep this money. It comes from Satan and I shall not touch it."

When the reverend was out the door for the second time the council members sat shaking their heads knowing that they had made the right decision.

One Week Later

Reverend Brantley was in his small rental apartment over a garage in Mt. Dora Florida when his phone rang. "Hello, Reverend Brantley speaking."

"Reverend, this is nurse Brubaker from your mother's nursing home. She has taken a turn for the worst and is requesting that you come to see her as soon as possible. I wish you would hurry as I think she has little time left."

"I will be there within the hour," the reverend replied.

Brantley went twice a month to see his mother at the home. He would have gone more often but he was always taken aback by the smells and sounds of the elderly housed there waiting to die. He always wished there would be a more dignified way to take care of his seventy-six-year-old dying mother, but he was in no financial position to help. His father had also passed away in the same home four years earlier.

He entered his mother's room, sat down in a chair by the bed and took her hand. She opened her eyes upon feeling his hand and smiled. "I am glad you could make it, William. I have something very important to tell you. Something I have been holding back since the day you were born."

"What is it, Mother?"

"It is so hard to tell you this but I feel the Lord is calling me and don't have much time left. William, I am not your birth mother. Your father and I had tried to have a child for a number of years but were unsuccessful. We sought medical help and found out I could never have children. That's when we decided to adopt a child. That child was you. We almost told you a couple of times but we were afraid we would lose you."

Brantley couldn't find words to say at first and just stared at his mother. Finally he spoke, "Do you know who my birth mother is?"

"William, your mother died in giving birth to twin boys in Orlando, Florida. She was an unwed teen and had five brothers and sisters. Her parents were very poor and could not afford to raise two more children. So they put the twins up for adoption."

"You said twins. Do you mean I have a twin brother?"

"Yes, William. Your brother was adopted by a family in the military. Their name was Whitehead and I believe they were stationed at an air force base in Tampa. We only met them briefly on the day we were allowed to take you home from the hospital. I believe it is called the Orlando Regional Medical Center now. I wish I could tell you more but that is all the information we were allowed."

"Thank you for telling me this, Mother. I always thought you were my mother and I will continue to think so. Also, I always felt that part of me was missing and now, knowing I have a twin brother, I know where the feeling came from. I will have to find him."

He thanked his mother for telling him the truth, kissed her on the hand and cheek and left.

Brantley sat in his apartment and pondered the first step in trying to locate his long lost brother. He knew it would be futile to do a people search online as he had no city or state to narrow it down. He knew his birth date:

November 21, 1961. He also knew that his brother's adoptive parents were stationed at a military base in Tampa. That had to be the Mac Dill Air Force Base. He figured the best approach was to contact the Veterans Administration to see if they had information on a person by the name of Whitehead stationed there at that time.

He typed in Veterans Administration in the Yahoo search engine. This led to a site called Military.com which was a free site used to locate your military buddies. He thought he would give it a try. He typed in all the pertinent information he knew and clicked on the search button.

The names and addresses of two Whiteheads appeared. One was Walter Whitehead residing in The Villages, Florida. The other was a Harold Whitehead from Canton, Ohio. He said aloud to himself, "Isn't the Internet wonderful!"

He called information and found the phone number for Harold Whitehead in Canton, Ohio and dialed. He was trembling with anticipation when an elderly lady answered the phone.

"This is the Whitehead residence."

"Hello, this is Reverend Brantley from Ocala, Florida. I was wondering if I could have a minute of your time. Is Harold available?"

"Oh, I am sorry but Harold is in the hospital."

"I am so sorry to hear that, is this Mrs. Whitehead?"

"Yes, it is."

"Perhaps you could help me then. I am looking for an old Air Force buddy. Was your husband stationed at the Mac Dill Air Force base in 1961?"

"Yes, I think he was around that time."

"Were you there with him?"

"Oh, no. That was before we were married."

"I see. Then you would not have adopted a child in Orlando, Florida in 1961."

"Heavens, no. We have four children of our own."

"Well, thank you, Mrs. Whitehead. You have been a great help. I hope your husband gets better soon. Goodbye."

"Goodbye."

Brantley was almost one hundred percent certain that Walter Whitehead from The Villages was the person he was looking for. Rather than call he thought it would be best to pay a personal visit since they lived so close. In fact, less than twenty-five miles from the central Florida community.

The Villages is a planned retirement community with over sixty villages. It is the largest age restricted adult community in the world. Each village has a town center which is the activity center of the village. The golf cart is the transportation method of choice in The Villages. Cart paths follow all the paved roads and have the right of way. Customized golf carts can be seen parked by the hundreds at all businesses and parking lots.

Brantley arrived in The Villages in the early afternoon. He had to stop at the guard house of The Rio Grande Village while they contacted the Whiteheads. Being a gated community he could not just drive up to the house and knock on the door. The guard contacting the Whiteheads said they wanted to know what he wanted with them. They weren't expecting a visit from a reverend. He asked the guard if he could hand him the phone so he could talk to them.

The guard handed him the phone stating Mrs. Whitehead was on the line.

"Hello, Mrs. Whitehead?

"Yes. This is she."

"This is Reverend Brantley from up in Ocala. I need to talk to you about a matter that has to do with when Mr. Whitehead was stationed at Mac Dill in 1961."

"That was a very long time ago. What could you possibly want now?"

"It is very important, Mrs. Whitehead, and I don't want to discuss it over the phone."

"Oh, alright. Hand the phone back to the guard and I'll tell him to let you through."

"Thank you, Mrs. Whitehead."

The guard gave him directions to La Jolla Circle and pushed the button to lift the gate to let him through. Brantley, after managing to avoid all the golf carts, pulled his old Subaru into the driveway of the courtyard villa home, walked to the front door, and knocked. Mrs. Whitehead answered the door, and looking utterly confused, asked if he was the reverend. He said he was. She said she thought he was her son and with a continued look of confusion on her face invited him in.

Walter appeared from the garage door after just coming home from the golf course. The Whiteheads used their golf cart for everyday transportation. Walter's golf cart was parked in the garage. "Franklin, about time you come for a visit."

Mrs. Whitehead said, "Walter. It's not Franklin. It's Reverend Brantley from Ocala."

"I don't understand. He's the spittin' image of Franklin."

The reverend began, "I know what I want to talk to you about happened a long time ago but it is something that greatly affects me. I was recently told by my mother that I was adopted as a newborn in Orlando, Florida in 1961. She also said that another newborn was adopted on the same day by a couple named Whitehead. Are you that couple?"

The Whiteheads spoke in unison, "Yes, we are!" Mrs. Whitehead continued, "That's when we brought Franklin home. It was one of the happiest days of our lives."

Reverend Brantley asked, "Does Franklin know he was adopted?"

"Oh, yes. We told him when he was still quite young. We didn't think it would be fair to keep it from him."

"Did you tell him he had a twin brother?"

"Oh my, no! We didn't know. They didn't tell us at the hospital. Are you trying to say you are Franklin's twin brother?"

"Yes, I am. I would like to get in touch with him. Would you tell me where I can find him? "

"He is living up in Jacksonville. I'll call him right away and tell him the news."

"I wish you wouldn't, Mrs. Whitehead. I would like to go see him personally and tell him. I think this should be just between brothers."

The Whiteheads agreed to go along with his wishes. They asked him all kinds of questions about his life and they gave him a short history of Franklin's. He received

Franklin's address and phone number, and before he was on his way Mrs. Whitehead hugged him. "Today I have been blessed with another son."

"Oh, one other thing, Mrs. Whitehead. Do you happen to know the name of our birth mother?"

"Yes, her name was Nancy Bixler. But I should tell you that she passed away giving birth to you and your brother."

"Yes, I know about her passing. I just wanted to know her name in case we want to locate some of our relatives. I assume they were from the Orlando area?"

"I believe so. I am sorry, but that is all the information we have to give."

"Thank you, Mrs. Whitehead. You have been a great help. I will tell Franklin you said hello. Goodbye."

Chapter 10

May, 2009

Reverend Brantley was driving back from the Villages when his cell phone rang. He fumbled for the phone and managed to answer it without running off the road.

"Reverend Brantley speaking."

"Reverend, this is nurse Brubaker again. I am sorry to give you this bad news, but your mother took a sudden turn for the worst and passed away a half hour ago. I went into her room after you left this morning and she said that after talking with you she was ready to go to the Lord and be with her husband, Marvin. She said you would understand."

"Yes. I do understand, nurse Brubaker. She had something to get off her mind. Now she is at peace. I'll start making the arrangements as soon as I get home."

Having to put the contact with his brother on hold the reverend called the Benson Crematorium to make arrangements for his mother's cremation. It was their known wish for his parents to be cremated and their ashes to be spread together on the ocean off Key West where they spent their honeymoon. It was the least he could do for them after raising him and putting him through seminary college.

He also made a call to the law firm of Begley and Hart to inform them of his mother's passing; the law firm was the executor of his mother's will. Mr. Begley told him to inform the firm when his parents' wishes had been carried out. He said it was a stipulation of the will that the reading would take place only after the ashes were confirmed to have been spread as requested.

Mrs. Brantley's remains were cremated three days after her death. The reverend found the large urn that contained his father's ashes next to the fireplace in his mother's house; the house appeared to have been undisturbed during the six months that his mother was in the nursing home. He also had made arrangements with a mowing service to keep the yard in shape to give the house a lived-in appearance.

Reverend Brantley poured his mother's ashes from the Styrofoam container he received from the crematorium into the large urn containing his father's ashes. After strapping the urn into the rear seatbelt of his aging Subaru he was off to Key West.

The four hundred and fifty mile trip took him nine hours to complete and he arrived quite late at the Ramada. He had made arrangements with a small charter fishing boat to take him offshore in the morning.

He arrived at the dock at eight AM sharp and met the charter captain. The captain was in a good mood as the minimum charter was a half day and this trip would only last one hour at the most. The captain did have to sign an affidavit stating that the ashes were spread as requested. Brantley also bought a disposable camera to document the dispersal of the ashes for the law firm.

When the boat reached the offshore five mile point the captain put the inboard engine in idle. Brantley checked the wind direction to assure none of the ashes would be blown back onto him and the boat. The captain took the pictures of Brantley releasing the ashes and of the rapidly disappearing trace on the water's surface. Back onshore an hour later the affidavit was signed by the captain and Brantley headed back to central Florida.

With all the stipulations met, Lawyer Begely held the reading of the will two days after Brantley returned from Key West. Brantley almost fell off his chair when he found out he was the heir to a sizable amount of money in addition to the property and life insurance. He always thought his parents were not financially well off as they were very frugal and made every dime count, yet the entire estate he inherited was in excess of one and a half million dollars.

The Reverend Brantley was sitting in his parents' home, which was now his, pondering what he would do with his newfound wealth. He was tired of being tied down to the job of minister of a single church. The money would give him the freedom to start a traveling ministry and hold tent revivals wherever a church needed his services.

He thought about how he would travel and stay on the road for perhaps six months at a time. He knew he didn't like staying in motels with all the noise of people coming and going especially the noisy children and pets. He decided to visit the local RV dealer.

The salesman did a good job of selling the RV lifestyle and sold the reverend a new Montana fifth wheel trailer. The next step was to purchase a truck to tow it. He traded his old Subaru in on a new Ford super duty truck the same afternoon.

With all the happenings of the last two weeks out of the way he was once again free to contact his brother. He decided to drive his new RV rig up to Jacksonville and contact his brother when he got there. He didn't want to call ahead as he wanted the first contact to be a face to face meeting. He was taught in seminary school to heighten the drama in his sermons. What could be more dramatic than meeting his twin brother for the first time face to face, especially for his brother who didn't know he existed?

The reverend confirmed a reservation in the Briarwood RV Park in south Jacksonville near Interstate 95. The park also included a section for mobile homes.

Franklin Whitehead just happened to be renting one of those mobile homes. Brantley learned from Franklin's adoptive parents that he was divorced from his wife after eleven years of marriage. Of course she got the house in the University District and he was forced to live in the trailer park.

The reverend was lucky to obtain a pull thru site at the front of the RV park. He had not had time to practice backing up his rig into a site before he left on his first RV trip. This was something he made a mental note to do. Perhaps in a large parking lot.

He was fumbling with the sewer hose connection when the park super saw he was having trouble.

"This your first time out, Mr. Brantley?

"Yes it is. How did you guess? They showed me how to do all these hookups at the dealer but it must have gone in one ear and out the other."

"I'll lend you a hand," the super said. "I'm sure you'll have this all down pat in no time. Sure is a nice rig you got here."

"Well, thank you, sir. Your help is greatly appreciated."

"Say, you look just like a feller that lives in one of the house trailers out back. In fact you look close enough to be his twin."

"You are correct, friend. I am here to pay him a surprise visit. If you happen to see him before I do, please don't mention that I am here."

"Oh, don't worry. I wouldn't want to spoil your surprise."

After hooking up his RV to the site, the reverend sat in his trailer trying to think of the best way to approach his brother. "Should I call first or just walk up to his door and knock? Imagine his expression when he sees me. Imagine my expression when I see him. I think I'll call his number to make sure he is home before I go knock."

Brantley dialed Franklin's number and his brother answered, "Hello."

"Hello, is this Franklin Whitehead?

"Speaking, who's calling?

"This is Reverend Brantley from down in Ocala. I have something very important I need to see you about. Is now a good time? I am right here in the RV park."

"What's the nature of your business? You're not a Jehovah's Witness are you?"

"No, nothing like that. You will know the nature of my business as soon as you see me."

"Well, OK. Come on down. I have a few minutes."

"Thank you, Mr. Whitehead. You won't regret it."

The reverend walked back through the park and found Franklin's house trailer on Avenue B. He walked up the short set of stairs to the treated wood deck and knocked.

Franklin answered the door and said, "Reverend Brantley?" Then his jaw dropped and he couldn't manage any more words as he stared at the reverend.

Brantley said with a waiver in his voice, "Franklin, I am your brother."

"My brother? I don't understand. I don't have a brother."

"Please, let me in so we can sit down and I'll explain it all to you."

Franklin said numbly, "Yes. Please come on in."

Franklin had to clear a place for the reverend to sit. The inside of the trailer had all the earmarks of a recently divorced bachelor's pad. Dishes stacked in the sink, clothes hung over chairs, and an empty pizza box on the coffee table.

"I'm sorry about how this place looks. I am recently divorced and haven't learned to pick up after myself yet."

Brantley said, "I'm sure you'll get the hang of it. I've lived by myself for a number of years and just recently decided to keep my own place in order. It does make you feel better about yourself and gives you a better outlook on life."

"Now, Reverend, what is this all about, and explain to me how you are my brother."

"Franklin, you are not only my brother, you are my twin brother. Our mother was an unwed teen named Nancy Bixler. Unfortunately, she died giving birth to us. Her family was dirt poor and she had five other siblings. Her parents couldn't afford to raise two more children so they put us up for adoption. You were adopted by the Whiteheads and I was adopted by the Brantleys. I guess it was easier to split us up then for someone to adopt twins."

"How did you find all this out? My parents told me I was adopted but they didn't tell me I had a twin brother."

"The Whiteheads didn't know about me. Somehow the Brantleys found out. The Brantleys never told me I was adopted until recently. In fact my mother, Mrs. Brantley, informed me on her deathbed. She told me that you were adopted by a couple named Whitehead stationed at Mac Dill. I was then able to track down your adoptive parents who live in the Villages. Mrs. Whitehead gave me your address and phone number and so here I am."

"Well, Reverend, I guess it's true then. I don't believe it. I mean I do believe it. I have a twin brother! Damn looking at you is just like looking into a mirror."

The two brothers spent the next few hours bringing each other up to date on their lives. Franklin told how he joined the army right out of high school and decided to make a career out of it. He became a demolition expert and served in the first Gulf War where he managed to find and destroy countless land mines without blowing himself up.

Franklin became extremely vocal against the "Don't ask Don't Tell" policy when it was implemented by the armed forces. The policy was to prevent military personnel from discriminating or harassing gay members as long as they remain closeted. His superiors became weary of his tirades against the policy and under the guise of downsizing gave him an honorable discharge from the army three years shy for his twenty year retirement pay. However he joined the army reserves and could be eligible for some retirement pay at age sixty.

His full time military career being over, Franklin found a position with the Jacksonville Sheriff's Office Bomb Squad; he had held for the last fourteen years.

His marriage at age thirty-seven into a prominent Jacksonville family didn't stand the test of time as his divorce was final five months ago. She grew weary of the stress in not knowing if he would return home in one piece after he left for work in the morning. His wife finally gave in to the wishes of his in-laws for her to end the marriage. His brother-in-law had come out of the closet and announced his relationship with his male partner two years previously. Franklin's dislike of the "Don't Ask Don't Tell" policy that got him booted out of the army had given him a hard time accepting his gay brother-in-law. Making his position known every chance he got didn't sit too well with his wife or her family, hence the divorce.

Brantley said his history wasn't as glamorous as Franklin's as he had chosen a more sedate life. After high school he spent a few years in limbo not knowing which direction to take. As his adoptive parents were deeply religious people they were ecstatic when he finally decided to enroll in the Florida Christian College in Kissimmee.

He was nearly expelled from the school when a small group of students, including Brantley, were accused of beating up a fellow student they determined was gay. The student didn't press charges and consequently the incident was overlooked by the school administration. The student who received the beating left the school, enrolled in a Catholic seminary, and eventually became a Catholic priest.

After college Brantley volunteered for missionary work in South America. He then served as a junior minister in a number of large Christian churches before obtaining his own ministry. He was never able to land a position in one of the larger churches and so led a fairly Spartan life as minister of a few small churches in Florida. His last position in Mt. Dora had not worked out well at all. He told Franklin about his dismissal from the church and how they wanted to invite the gay community for services.

With the inheritance from his mother he was ready to pursue his lifelong dream of conducting a traveling ministry where he could preach as he liked. He was sure there were many churches that would accept his style.

When the reverend was finished Franklin said, "Well, brother, it looks like we are of one mind as far as the gay community is concerned. It doesn't surprise me at all that we would have things in common, being identical twins."

Chapter 11

May 2009

Reverend Billy Brantley and his newfound twin brother, Franklin Whitehead, just had the reunion of their lives. Their first meeting lasted well past midnight as they brought each other up to speed on their life histories. They mutually came to the conclusion that they should look up the rest of their family members. According to their adoptive mothers they were from the Orlando area and the family name was Bixler.

Franklin had some vacation time coming from the sheriff's department so as soon as he could get it cleared he and Billy would head down to Orlando to begin the search. They decided to take the Montana fifth wheel for the trip. They figured they could get better acquainted with each other in the RV and campground environment. Brantley also needed practice in handling the big fifth wheel camper. Franklin would be a great help in giving Billy directions for backing the rig into a site.

While Franklin was arranging to take his vacation Brantley busied himself with shopping for additional items needed in the camper. He bought a set of silverware, pots and pans, sheets, blankets, and pillows. He also went grocery shopping to stock the pantry and refrigerator. He had decided to temporarily use items from the house he inherited from his parents but would replace them when he returned home.

While in Orlando the reverend would also check in with some fellow preachers he knew from college. He wanted to get advice on starting his evangelical tent revival career. Perhaps they just might give him a break and sponsor him for a revival at one of their churches.

Brantley had made reservations for Monday at the Winter Garden RV Resort which was located on the west side of Orlando. He figured this was the general area in which his extended family might be located.

Early on Monday the brothers were on the road heading south and reached the campground in late afternoon. The only site available was a tight back in site, and Billy had quite a bit of trouble backing in. After repeated attempts and finally getting a feel as to which way to turn the truck's steering wheel he finally positioned the trailer in a suitable location. "Well, Frankie, I think this was about the worst it could get. From now on it's all downhill. That sure was frustrating but invaluable practice."

"Yeah, I could see your face getting red, Billy. I even thought I heard you curse once. Not good for a preacher. Maybe next time you should save your soul and ask for a pull through site," Franklin said with a grin.

"Maybe your right, brother."

After all the hookups were made and they were settled in they logged on to the campgrounds WI-FI system and checked the online white pages for Bixlers. There were two listed for Wintergarden and two listed for Ocoee.

Brantley decided to call the Wintergarden numbers first. He received an answer on the first try.

"Hello, Bixlers' residence."

"Is this Mrs. Bixler?"

"Yes it is. What do you want?"

"This is Reverend Brantley from up in Ocala. I am looking for the relatives of a Miss Nancy Bixler who died in childbirth back in nineteen sixty-one. Would you be able to help me?"

"Oh my, that was a long time ago. I don't recall a Nancy in my husband's immediate family. Of course that would be a generation back. You might get some information from the Bixlers over in Ocoee. Try Walter Bixler. He is my husband's great uncle. He is quite old."

"Thank you, Mrs. Bixler. I found his number listed. Nice talking to you. Goodbye."

Brantley dialed the number for Walter Bixler. The phone rang nine times and he was about to hang up when a loud voice came on the line.

"HELLO."

"Yes, hello, is this Walter Bixler?

"I was the last time I woke up. You'll have to speak up. I don't hear that well anymore."

"Walter, this is Reverend Billy Brantley. I am looking for the relatives of a Nancy Bixler who passed away during childbirth in nineteen sixty-one. Would you be able to help me?"

"You could be referring to my brother, Charlie's girl. As I recall her name was Nancy. She did die quite young. I don't recall it was during childbirth. That was a funny family. They mostly kept to themselves."

"Do you know if any of Nancy's brothers or sisters are still in the area? They would be your nieces and nephews."

"I know who they would be. I didn't lose my mind entirely yet, young feller. The only one that comes to mind would be her sister, Irene. She married a fellow named Baxter, David Baxter. They live in Orlando. He's a lawyer."

"Do you happen to know their phone number?"

"No I don't. I gotta go. My soup is boiling over."

"OK, thank you Uncle Walter. Goodbye."

Brantley wondered if the feisty old gentleman caught on that he called him Uncle Walter.

The phone number for David Baxter was listed under Attorneys in Orlando. Brantley dialed the number and a receptionist answered.

"Baxter and Lewis Law Office."

"Hello. This is Reverend Billy Brantley. May I please speak with Mr. Baxter?

"Are you a client of his?"

"No I am not. This is a family matter."

"Just a minute, I'll see if he is free."

After a minute the attorney came on the line, "Hello, David Baxter speaking."

"Mr. Baxter, this is Reverend Billy Brantley. I need to talk to your wife, Irene, about an urgent family matter. I would like to meet at your residence this evening if at all possible."

"Is there something I can help you with over the phone?"

"I am afraid not. It concerns your wife's side of the family and I would prefer to talk directly with her. My business is legitimate and is in no way negative or harmful to Mrs. Baxter."

"Well, I guess you can stop by at about seven-thirty. We should be finished with dinner by then. Do you have our address?"

"No, I am afraid I don't."

Baxter gave Brantley the address and reaffirmed the time for the seven-thirty meeting.

Brantley programmed the address into his GPS and arrived at the Baxter's posh residence in Baldwin Park right on time. The brothers walked up the brick driveway and rang the bell. A regal looking lady in her mid-sixties answered the door and was taken slightly aback at the sight of the twin brothers.

"Reverend Brantley?"

"Yes, I am Reverend Brantley, and this is my brother, Franklin Whitehead. Are you Irene Baxter?"

"Yes I am," she replied with tear brimmed eyes. "I know who you boys are. I can see the family resemblance. You must be my sister Nancy's boys. I knew the last names of the couples who adopted you both. I find it hard to believe. After all these years we will finally get to meet you. Welcome home. Please come in."

Mr. Baxter took his wife aside and spoke in a low tone, "Don't move too fast into this, Irene. You know what happened the last time."

"Oh, I know David, but this time it's real. I Just know it."

They all set in the expansive living room and Mrs. Baxter served sweet tea.

After telling once again their life stories to their Aunt Irene and hearing her tell about their extended family, Brantley asked the question that was foremost in his mind.

"Aunt Irene, do you know who our father is?"

A look of great concern came over her as she glanced at her husband. Mr. Baxter told her, "You might as well go ahead and tell them. They will probably find out on their own anyway."

"Boys, this has been a family secret all of our lives. I don't know just how to tell you but to come right out with the truth. Our Uncle James—who is your grandfather's youngest brother–was only five years older than your mother. He and your mother had a close relationship. Just how close we didn't know until she announced she was pregnant and we found out it was to him."

Billy and Franklin, taken aback by the news said in near unison, "You mean our great Uncle James is also our father?"

"I am sorry you boys had to find out something like this, but it is the truth. Her uncle being your father plus the near poverty-level condition of our family were the two main reasons you two were put up for adoption. They also didn't want to be faced with the stigma of having an incestuous affair known outside the family. We always wondered where you were and if we would ever get to meet you, but now here you are. I am so glad."

Franklin asked, "Is our father still alive?"

David Baxter answered, "Uncle James lives over in Zephyrhills in a mobile home community. I can give you his address and phone number, but first you have to submit a sample for a DNA test."

"Why should we have to do that?" Franklin asked.

"We need to verify you are who you say you are before you can claim the trust fund."

"What in the world are you talking about? What trust fund?"

"Your grandfather, Charles Bixler, died eight years ago. Nine years ago he won the Florida lottery to the extent of fourteen million dollars. Of course after taking the lump sum amount and tax withholding the bottom line amount was nine million. Knowing he only had a short time to live he shared his winnings with all of his family and known grandchildren. He always felt guilt for putting his two newborn grandchildren up for adoption forty-nine years ago, so he created a trust fund in the names of John and Joe Doe. The trust fund is to be divided among the rest of his family if a legal claim was not made during a ten year period. We have had several fraudulent claims, but with having to be subjected to a DNA test the claims were dropped rather quickly. Knowingly submitting a false claim would be committing a felony and punishable by law."

Brantley asked what the trust funds were worth.

"The amount will only be divulged after positive DNA test results. But I can say it is well worth your time. I am the attorney handling the matter. Tomorrow I will set up an appointment at the lab where you need to be tested. It is right here in Orlando."

Brantley asked his brother if he was up for the test.

"I sure am," Franklin replied. "Maybe I can move out of that darn trailer and get some decent accommodations. Of course my ex will probably lay claim to half of it. But we'll cross that bridge when we come to it."

Franklin and Billy gave their DNA samples the next day and were told that the results would be forwarded to Baxter's law office. The testing would take at least two days.

During the wait for the test results Brantley contacted two friends from college that held ministerial positions at Orlando churches. He sought their advice as to his plans to operate a traveling ministry and asked if they could help in any way to get him started. Reverend Brennan from the Episcopal Church told him about a church in Crystal Springs near Zephyrhills that had a tent revival scheduled for Saturday evening but the minister had to cancel because of illness. Brennan told Billy that he would make the call to the Crystal Springs church on his behalf. Brantley might be able to fill in for the ill preacher.

One hour later Brantley received a call from a Reverend Simms from the First Baptist Church in Crystal Springs. Brantley told Simms about his plans for starting a traveling ministry and that he would be willing to cover for the ill preacher at no cost to the church. Since he came recommended by Reverend Brennan, Simms accepted the offer. Brantley was ecstatic that his new career would begin Saturday night. He firmly believed the Lord was showing him the way and providing the means.

On Thursday afternoon Brantley received a call from Baxter's law office asking the brothers to stop in as soon as possible. They arrived at the lawyer's office just after 3:00 P.M.

The receptionist led them right in to Baxter's office.

"Gentlemen, have a seat, please. I have some very good news for you. Your tests came back 99.99% positive when your DNA samples were tested against your Uncle James and Aunt Irene. The results would stand up in any court of law as to your being the sons of Nancy Bixler and James Bixler. Welcome to the family. Now if you would just read and sign these two documents you will be the rightful owners of the aforementioned trust funds."

Billy and Franklin both reached for the documents and started reading. Billy's only reaction was a contented smile and a glance to heaven when he saw the bottom line amount of the trust fund in excess of seven hundred thousand dollars each. Franklin, however, upon seeing the bottom line started shaking and uttered an only slightly intelligible "Holy shit."

After the documents were signed Baxter told the brothers how the funds could be accessed. He would give them a signed authorization to take to the bank and he would personally call the bank manager to inform him of the resolution of the trusts. They could go to the bank the next day to have the funds transferred to accounts of their choice or to establish new accounts at the bank.

Franklin then asked for the address and phone number of James Bixler, their father and great uncle. Baxter told them where James was living and also stated that he had a son named Calvin who lived with him also. Baxter told them to be careful how they approached James and Calvin as it was Calvin who had attempted one of the unsuccessful fraudulent attempts to gain the trust funds.

He related how Calvin made a deal with a set of twins that had a slight family resemblance. The twins agreed to a seventy/thirty split of the funds for their efforts. However they hightailed it upon learning of the DNA test requirement. Baxter also told them that Calvin suffered from a Dissociative Identity Disorder, commonly referred to as DID or multiple personalities and that he could be quite unpredictable at times.

The brothers thanked Baxter and said they would take their chances with their stepbrother and cousin, Calvin.

Franklin and Billy met with the bank manager Friday morning and signed the paperwork to have the trusts account names changed from John and Joe Doe to their actual names. Franklin gave the bank manager the account and routing numbers of his bank account in Jacksonville and was told that the funds would be transferred within two days. Brantley said he would be in touch at a later date as to the transference of his funds.

Three hours later they were on their way towing the fifth wheel to a campground in Zephyrhills.

Chapter 12

May 2009 – Zephyrhills, Florida

The brothers arrived at the Hillcrest RV Resort in Zephyrhills in early afternoon. They motored up to the sign that read all "RVs stop here to register." Billy went into the office and requested a pull-through site. The young female clerk said she had a nice wide pull through available near the pool. Billy registered and paid for the site, then following the campground map, found it, and eased his rig into it. On one side of them was a forty-foot Tiffen class A motor home and a Fleetwood thirty-foot travel trailer was on the other side. The site had a nice concrete pad and a picnic table that wasn't falling apart. Billy said, "A lot can be said for nice level pull-through sites; setup should be a breeze."

Franklin replied, "It better be a breeze, after all we are in Zephyrhills."

Billy just smiled at his brother and slowly shook his head.

After a light lunch of ham and cheese sandwiches, chips, and soft drinks in the trailer they followed the GPS to the Wood Dale Mobil Home Park. The park was small, and the ancient mobile home units were tightly packed with only small patches of sparse grass between them. They found their father's unit on Boston Ave., lot number 18 at the end of the avenue. It was one of the few double wides with some shade trees.

A man of about their same age was on a small deck grilling three hotdogs on a rusty old gas grill. Franklin marveled at the close family resemblance with himself and Billy. The man watched the brothers as they exited the truck and he spoke to them, saying: "Aunt Irene called and said you guys would probably be coming around. You should have called first. I would have gone out and bought a few more dogs."

"Don't worry about that," Franklin replied. "We already had lunch. You must be our stepbrother, Calvin."

"In the flesh," Calvin replied.

Just then a voice shouted from the inside of the house, "Calvin, are those dogs ready yet? I'm hungry. And who in hell are you talking to out there?"

"Just two of your long lost sons, Dad."

There was a long moment of silence inside the double wide home then the screen door slowly opened and James Bixler stepped out onto the deck. He looked older than his seventy years of age: unshaven gray stubble, dressed in an old yellowing t-shirt and stained and torn gray shorts. He stared and squinted at the two brothers then said, "You boys mean nothing to me. They never let me see you when you was born, and they never would tell me where you went. I just put it in my mind that you didn't exist and I still feel the same way now. Calvin, bring my hotdog in." And with that said their father went back into his double wide trailer with the wooden screen door slamming shut behind him.

Calvin took the hotdog into his father and moments later returned outside to the deck. "I am sorry about our father, but he has other reasons to be angry."

"What would those reasons be?" Franklin asked.

"As I guess you found out there was over one and a half million dollars in your trust funds that was due to be distributed among the family in about a year if you didn't show up. My father and I figured we would receive a portion of it now that Uncle Charles is dead. We figured to inherit about two hundred thousand. Now that won't happen. I am afraid our father would rather have the money than two additional sons."

"I guess that's why he was not overjoyed to see us," Brantley said. "Calvin, our Aunt Irene mentioned something I would like to talk to you about."

"Oh, and what did the old girl have to say?"

"She said you were suffering from some sort of mental disorder, and I may be able to help. Have you been to a doctor about it?"

"Yeah, I've been to a psychiatrist and he said I suffer from a multiple personality disorder. I think mental problems run in the family. We are an odd bunch."

"Have you been taking any medication for it?"

"I had a prescription for some anti-depressants but when they ran out I couldn't afford to refill it. The psychiatrist tried to get me to start psychotherapy but we couldn't afford that either. My dad is living off Social Security and I receive a small disability check. With the economy the way it is and with my condition I haven't been able to hold down a full-time job with any health insurance benefits. Just a couple of odd jobs here and there."

"I have no sympathy for our father, and contrary to some verses in the Bible, I believe the sins of the father should not be paid for by the son. I will write you out a check right now for two hundred thousand dollars but you must promise to once again seek psychiatric care and take the proper medicine for your condition. Please don't think of it as charity. It is your rightful inheritance from your Uncle Charles."

Calvin excitedly said, "You said you would make the check out to me. What about our father?"

"It's up to you whether or not you tell your father. It seems your Uncle Charles held a long time grudge against his younger brother for what he did to his daughter, Nancy. Incest is not particularly well thought of in the Bible. In fact, in Leviticus sexual relations between close relatives is strictly forbidden by God. I think your Uncle Charles had a very good reason not to include your father in the monetary disbursement of his lottery winnings. But like I said before, the sins of the father should not be borne by the son."

"I guess I can accept your conditions," Calvin replied.

Franklin spoke up, "Billy do you want me to chip in for the two hundred thousand?"

"That's not necessary, Franklin. I received a generous inheritance from my adoptive mother and have more than enough money to finance my evangelical mission."

As Brantley was writing out the check for Calvin he invited him to attend his first tent revival meeting down in Crystal Springs. With a smile he let him know it was not another condition of the inheritance but he would appreciate it if he would attend.

Calvin accepted the check and told Billy he would be delighted to attend. He had never been to a revival let alone to church in the last thirty years. "It'll be refreshing to get away from my old man for a while. He can be a real pain in the ass sometimes."

Neither Billy nor Franklin mentioned Calvin's attempt to illegally claim the trust fund. They gave him the benefit of the doubt because of his mental condition and the negative influence of their father.

Billy had a six o'clock meeting about the Saturday revival with Reverend Simms down in Crystal Springs. Franklin said he would rather be dropped off at the trailer than tag along. While Billy was gone Franklin said he intended to research their stepbrother's mental condition on the Internet.

Franklin found an abundance of information on Dissociative Identity Disorder on medical related web sites. He learned that in the majority of the cases the patients suffered from a traumatic event during their childhood. Many times they were the victims of severe physical and sexual abuse during early or mid-childhood. The memories and feelings of the abuse are forced into the subconscious but can be brought back in the conscious state of a separate personality.

The patient can experience multiple beliefs with each personality with those beliefs being polar opposite from each other. Patients can suffer from depression and sudden unjustified angry periods. Psychotherapy along with medication for depression if present is the most used and most successful treatment.

Franklin thought about calling up his Aunt Irene to question her about Calvin's upbringing but then reconsidered. He figured there was enough disruption in their newfound family in the last week. It could wait for another time.

He also wondered what Calvin would do with the two hundred grand his brother had given him. Which personality would surface to control the newfound wealth and would he actually go seek psychiatric help?

Billy returned from the meeting in Crystal Springs shortly after eight o'clock. Franklin told him about his research of Calvin's mental illness and said it might have been a mistake to give him all the money at once.

"He seems all right now but we haven't seen him when the other personality takes over," Franklin said.

Billy said, "Franklin, you might be right, but now we can only hope for the best and pray for him."

The Saturday evening tent revival went extremely well for Brantley. Calvin managed to show up and seemed impressed and spiritually moved during the program. Brantley noticed from his position at the lectern that Calvin seemed to mentally drift away when he was expounding on his favorite subjects from the book of Leviticus.

Reverend Simms heartily thanked Brantley for volunteering to step in and give an excellent performance on such short notice. Brantley asked if he could use Reverend Simms as a reference for future revivals. Simms assured him that he would be happy to give him an excellent recommendation. He said in fact that he would like Brantley to leave an opening in his schedule for a return visit the same time next year. Brantley assured him he would.

Brantley spotted his stepbrother Calvin talking with Franklin at the edge of the parking lot and walked over.

"Calvin, what did you think of the revival?"

"I thought it was very moving, Billy. Sure is different having a preacher for a brother. Reverend Simms invited me to tomorrow's services, and I think I'll take him up on it."

"That's great, Calvin. That is what a revival is designed to do. To reignite one's faith and get him back into the folds of a church. Tonight's revival is already a success!"

"I'm gonna have to get rid of my old junker of a pickup if I have to drive down here to church. I barely made it here tonight. Had to stop and add a quart of oil."

"I think you can afford to upgrade your transportation now. You need a dependable car to get to your doctor also."

The brothers shook hands and went their separate ways. On their way back to Zephyrhills Franklin said he had to get back up to Jacksonville by Sunday night as he had to get back to work on Monday morning. He also had to contact his divorce attorney about the ramifications of his inheritance. Billy said it was no problem; they would head north first thing after breakfast. "I think it's your turn to cook Frankie."

Chapter 13

Zephyrhills, Florida - May 2009

Calvin slowly made his way back from Crystal Springs leaving a blue cloud of burning motor oil behind his aging gray Datsun pickup. He always kept a case of motor oil back in the bed and he had to pour another quart into the crankcase before he made it home to Zephyrhills. All the way back he was thinking about what kind of vehicle he would buy with the check from his stepbrother, Billy. The check was burning a hole in his wallet. It would definitely be another pickup. This time new. Maybe like his stepbrother's shiny new black F-250. "Yeah, that was a helluva truck," he murmured to himself.

Calvin made it home to the mobile home park at ten o'clock. His father was catching the night air out on the deck. "Where'ya been so long? I'm outta beer. You know the Quick Stop is too far fer me to hoof it."

"Well, just maybe the hike would do you some good."

"Don't sass me, boy. Now git back in that old heap o'yors and fetch me a six pack."

Calvin turned around and dutifully drove the half mile to the gas station and returned to his father. He slammed the six pack down on the small redwood table next to his father and entered the house. He barely heard his father say, "Careful with that, you little shit. You'll roon it."

Calvin drove into town on Monday morning to open an account at the First National Bank. He never did make it back to Crystal Springs for the Sunday worship service. Instead he spent the day Sunday thinking about what to do with the money Billy gave him. He made up his mind he was going to leave and let his old man fend for himself. He was tired of the abuse and constant ridicule. Hell, he was forty-seven years old. At least he hadn't tried to beat him since he was fifteen. But he wasn't going to tell him about the money. At least not just yet. He figured the old man would find out eventually and then he would have to admit to it.

Calvin showed the check to the bank teller and told her he wanted to open a checking and a savings account. The teller told him he had to wait for the assistant branch manager to finish up with another customer. While he was seated and waiting he paged thru an *Auto Trader* magazine and an ad caught his eye in the RV section.

For sale: 2008 F-250 Super Duty Diesel Truck
and 2008 Denali 5th Wheel travel
Trailer. Both with very low mileage.
$80K OBO. Call **********.

Calvin tore the page out of the magazine, folded it, and stuck it in his shirt pocket.

The assistant manager finally called him into her office and he filled out the necessary paperwork for the accounts. He was told the funds would be available in his accounts as soon as the large check cleared which should only take two days. She gave him a small pack of temporary checks and explained to him the online banking features available. And Calvin thought that online banking sounded like just the thing he needed to keep track of his money when traveling.

His next stop was Best Buy to purchase a new laptop computer and a prepaid cell phone. He thought he was near the fifteen hundred dollar limit of his credit card but the charges went through OK. He figured he would pay off the balance once his bank accounts were active and he was set up with the online banking.

The Best Buy technician showed him how to access the store's WI-FI and how to log onto his email. He told Calvin that if he was going to be permanently on the road he should open a Google or Yahoo email account. The accounts were free and with all the WI-FI hot spots available he could close out his regular Internet provider account. Calvin appreciated the advice and felt more than ever the itch to free himself from his domineering father.

Calvin sat in his truck and used his new cell phone to call the number listed on the ad for the truck and fifth wheel camper. An elderly sounding lady answered the phone. Calvin told her he was very interested in the truck and camper and that he would like to see it as soon as possible.

She told him her late husband had bought the rig in order for them to travel up to Minnesota and back to visit their children and grandchildren. But, unfortunately, they only made one trip before he passed away. She decided to sell it because she was not interested in learning how to handle it. She preferred to fly when she wanted to visit her kids and grandkids.

Calvin said he would like to see it that afternoon and told her not to sell it before he saw it. She told him not to worry about that as she had only received one other call and that had been three days ago. She said her name was Mrs. Harriet Wolf and gave Calvin her address up in Dade City. She said the rig was parked right out front with a for sale sign on it. She said her neighbor was helping her sell it and he would meet Calvin out front when he gets there. He should just toot his horn.

Calvin made the short trip to Dade City without adding oil to the Datsun. He spied the rig midway down the block and tooted his horn when he pulled into the drive.

The truck looked like it was in extremely good shape and the Denali fifth wheel looked even better. He was sitting behind the wheel of the F-250 when the neighbor appeared. "It's a beaut, isn't it?"

"It sure is," Calvin answered. "Do you have the keys?"

"Do you know how to start a diesel?"

"Yeah, I do. I drove one when I worked for a construction company."

The neighbor handed Calvin the keys and he inserted the key into the ignition. He turned the key the quarter turn to heat up the glow plugs. When the ready light came on he turned the key to the start position and the diesel came alive. He had never heard a sweeter sounding truck. Calvin looked around at the tan leather seats and the built in GPS and turned on a magnificent stereo. The odometer read only twelve thousand miles. Calvin thought, "Hardly broken in, and still some warranty left. Not even a scratch in the polished black exterior finish."

Next was a walkthrough of the twenty-eight foot fifth wheel. When Calvin stepped into the trailer he knew he had to have it. It was extremely clean with no pet smell. The living and kitchen areas were spacious with the slide extended. The front section had a queen size bed and an adequate corner shower. The closet was plentiful, especially for a single man. The clothes he owned would only fill up a small portion of the wardrobe.

Calvin knew he could live comfortably in the trailer. The only thing holding him back was the asking price. He knew he could buy a similar new rig for nearly the same amount. He asked the neighbor if the lady was firm on the price. He said he didn't know but that he could always make an offer; she wanted to sell pretty badly. She was talking about moving back up north with one of her kids.

Calvin knocked on Mrs. Wolf's door to make her an offer. He told her that with the collapse of the economy RV dealers were discounting new units to the bare bones and he could also get a good end of model year deal on a new truck. He told her he could only offer her fifty-thousand for the rig.

Her demeanor sagged when she heard the offer and said she would have to talk it over with her son. Calvin asked her if she was in possession of the titles. She said she was. He knew she didn't owe on the rig.

Calvin gave her his cell phone number and told her to call him when she made a decision. She said she would call him back in the morning.

Tuesday morning Calvin was on his way back from the Quick Stop with some egg and sausage biscuits for his father when his cell phone rang. He knew who was calling as he had given his new cell phone number to only one person. He pulled over to the side of the road and answered. It was Mrs. Wolf, the lady with the camper rig. She said she had talked it over with her son up in Minnesota and he advised her to go ahead and sell it to Calvin for fifty-thousand. He wanted her to move up with them as soon as possible.

Calvin said he would be up there in about two hours to give her a cash deposit. He had managed to put three hundred dollars aside that his dad didn't know about. He told Mrs. Wolf he would have to wait until Wednesday to get a cashier's check for the remainder. She said that would be fine.

That night after his father was passed out and in a deep sleep from the six pack that Calvin supplied him, he rummaged through the outdoor storage shed and found three old suit cases. All of his clothing and most of his personal possessions fit into the cases. The rest he packed into two cartons he picked up at the Quick Stop when he went for the beer. When everything was loaded into the Datsun he went to bed to rest up for the rest of his life, free from the abuse and ridicule of the old man.

Wednesday morning Calvin obtained a cashier's check for $49,700 payable to Mrs. Harriet Wolf. He had asked a neighbor kid to go with him up to Dade City in order to drive the Datsun back to the trailer park. He paid him twenty bucks for his troubles.

When his possessions were unloaded from the Datsun and piled next to the camper Calvin added another quart of oil to the crankcase to ensure that the kid could make it back to the trailer park with no problems.

After the kid was on his way Calvin presented the check to Mrs. Wolf and she gave him both of the titles, still in the State of Florida envelopes. The next door neighbor showed Calvin how to hook up the truck to the trailer and connect the 12-volt electrical line and he was all set.

He was surprised at the towing power of the truck. A few times on his way to the DMV to take care of the title transfer and tags he almost forgot he was towing the trailer.

Calvin figured he could call his father and tell him the news once he reached the campground near Ocala. Hell, if he didn't call the old man would probably have the police out looking for him.

Chapter 14

Late May 2009

Calvin was able to get a good monthly rate at the Live Oaks RV Park just south of Ocala. He was only fifty miles away from the old double wide and his father down in Zephyrhills, but it felt like he was a thousand miles away as he settled down into his new home and his newfound freedom. After a snack of sharp cheese on Ritz crackers and a longneck bottle of Icehouse beer he was ready to call his father to tell him the news.

His father answered after what seemed like the twentieth ring.

"Bixler's."

"This is Calvin."

"Calvin, where in hell are you? You know there's nuthin here for supper."

"Dad, you'll have to fend for yourself. I'm not coming home."

"Whadaya mean, you're not comin' home? Get your ass home here, boy."

"I left and I'm not coming back."

"How in hell can you leave? You don't have any money. Ya ain't gonna get far."

"I got all the money I need."

"Whadaya mean you got money? Where in hell did ya get money?

"That is none of your business."

"How much money do ya have? Whadya do, rob a bank?

"I said it was none of your business."

"You ungrateful sonovabitch. What am I gonna do for food? What in hell am I gonna do for supper?

"Father, I left the old pickup there for you. Go get your own supper for a change."

"I ain't gonna drive that old heap."

"Then call Meals on Wheels or find somebody else who can take your shit."

"Calvin this isn't the real you talking. Listen to reason and get home, ya hear?"

"Dad, this is the real me. The other Calvin that took all your shit no longer exists.

I am sorry for your loss. You are on your own now. Better get used to it quick."

His father started to protest, but Calvin hung up on him.

Calvin thought, *Boy that went well! What the hell, the old bastard got what he deserved.*

Calvin retrieved another bottle of Icehouse from his fridge and sat and thought about the call he had just made. His mind drifted back to the night his mother died, when he was six. He could still hear them arguing, and then from the hall he saw his father strike his mother. A backhand right across the face. He could still hear his mother's scream and see her fall. Her head struck the heavy ceramic cat doorstop by the front door. Then she was quiet and did not move.

His mother died in the hospital the next day from a brain hemorrhage. One of the ceramic cat's ears had penetrated her temple.

Calvin's father had verbally abused and demoralized him since.

He even blamed his mother's death on Calvin. He insisted that if she would not have stepped back onto his toy truck and had her feet go out from under her she would still be alive.

Calvin steeled himself against that memory and vowed he would shed the guilt he had carried since he was six. His mother died at his father's hand, not his.

The next day Calvin called his stepbrother, Billy, and told him he was in the area. Calvin told Billy how he left their father and of the abuse and guilt of his mother's death he had endured since he was six. Billy told him his leaving was for the best, and he should feel no guilt about his mother's death.

Calvin saw an ad posted in the campground office for a work camper on the maintenance crew. He applied and was hired to mow grass and do general repair work. Work campers get paid a small wage plus free RV site rental. Many full time RVers settle into the lifestyle when they get tired of being constantly on the move. With a little luck they can settle into an up-country area of their choice for an entire season, then head south for the winter. Calvin enjoyed the work. Even though the wages were small the money was enough for groceries and beer with no further outlay of money from his accounts.

Jacksonville, Late June, 2009

Franklin's life had been drastically improved with the turn of events from the previous month. His lawyer talked to his ex-wife's lawyer about the trust fund and his ex-wife and in-laws stated they wanted no part of him or his money. His ex-wife was doing just fine.

Franklin was doing just fine himself. He moved out of the old trailer park, bought a new Honda SUV and found a decent rental house in a new subdivision. He even started dating the blond real estate agent that handled the house rentals.

Franklin's cell phone rang as he stepped out of his new Honda, "Hello, Franklin Whitehead."

"Franklin, this is your Aunt Irene from down in Orlando. I am afraid I have some bad news for you."

"Go ahead Aunt Irene. What is it?"

"Your father passed away yesterday. Actually the police are sure it was suicide."

"What on earth did he do?"

"They said he hanged himself from the eave of his old storage shed. Bubba Bernstein, his neighbor, found him. We need you and your brothers to come down and make the arrangements. Ya'll are his closest kin. Just check with the police station when you come down. Do you know where Calvin is?"

"Yes I do, Aunt Irene. I'll contact my brothers and see how soon we can be there. Thanks for calling."

As soon as Franklin made it inside his house he called Billy and told him the news. Billy immediately thought of Calvin and how he would handle his father's death, especially the suicide part. He told Billy about Aunt Irene's request that they go down to Zephyrhills to make the arrangements. He said he would be ready to leave the next day as he could get an immediate three day leave for a death in the family. If he needed more time he still had additional accumulated vacation time to use. Billy told him he would have to talk to Calvin first and he would call Franklin back as soon as he could. Franklin said he would drive down to Ocala in the morning and they could all leave from there. Billy agreed and said Franklin could stay overnight at his place.

Calvin was out mowing at the RV park when Billy called, but he didn't hear his cell phone ring because of the loud drone of the mower. A half hour later when he took his break he checked his phone for missed calls and saw Billy's number. Since he had a semi-permanent address Calvin had signed on with Bellsouth. The pay as you go cell he had purchased at Best Buy ran short of minutes a week ago. He now had a brand new Nokia with all the gadgets including caller I.D.

He called Billy back from the coolness of his Denali. Billy told him the news about his father's suicide and that they would have to drive down to Zephyrhills to make the final arrangements. Billy thought it was kind of odd that Calvin showed very little reaction to the news. He just said he would be ready whenever Billy would. Billy said that Franklin was driving down to Ocala tomorrow and then they would leave the day after next. Calvin just said fine.

The three brothers made the one hour trip in Billy's truck. On the road they filled each other in on the happenings in their lives during the last month. Franklin only recently heard of Calvin's departure from their dad. He agreed that it was the best for Calvin. Calvin said his anxiety had lessened quite a bit in his new life and that medication was not necessary. He had one session with a psychiatrist in Ocala, at Billy's insistence, and the doc said that Calvin appeared perfectly normal.

Billy mentioned that his traveling ministry was beginning to look up. He had two revivals in Florida in September. He said churches in Florida rarely scheduled revivals during the dog days of summer. He would have to travel north into cooler climes for the summertime revivals.

Franklin told them about his ex's refusal of any of the trust fund money and that he had a new car, house, and a new love in his life. He was now dating the blond realtor who showed him the rental houses. Franklin was doing really well with the Jacksonville Sheriff's Office, too. He had been promoted to Sergeant in charge of the bomb squad just last week.

Billy had called his aunt the day before and said they would be coming down. The first stop was at the Zephyrhills police station. The detective in charge of the investigation said he was certain that their father's death was a suicide. There were no signs of a struggle or other wounds on the body. He said they would not have to I.D. the body as the neighbors already positively identified him as James Bixler at the scene.

Franklin asked how their father died. The detective asked if they wanted all the details and they said yes.

The detective went on to say that a neighbor by the name of Bubba saw the body at about seven in the morning when he was out walking his pit bull. He immediately called 911. I got the call and arrived at the scene about twenty minutes later. He was hanging from the eave of the old storage shed next to the house. I was surprised the old flower planter bracket took the weight. He used a length of green ten gauge electrical grounding wire. The noose was extremely strong. It looked like he stood on a short step ladder then kicked it out from under himself, and that was it. The ladder was laying on its side on the ground.

We checked inside the house and found a note on the kitchen table. It was addressed to his son Calvin. The detective handed Calvin the suicide note. Calvin accepted the note and read it aloud:

> "To my no good son, Calvin.
> My death is all your fault just
> like your mother's. I hope you
> enjoy the rest of your miserable
> life.
> Your father"

Calvin looked up after reading the note and said, "That old sonovabitch will probably still haunt me from his grave. I'll probably get a message from him that it's my fault the fire in hell is too hot."

Billy tried to stifle a chuckle but didn't succeed. The detective asked Calvin what his father meant about his mother's death. Calvin related the story of his mother's death when he was six years old.

The detective said that he heard from the neighbors that Calvin and his father were not getting along and that he left the area about a month ago. Calvin said that was correct that he moved up to Ocala. The detective then asked where Calvin was on Sunday night, the night of the suicide. Calvin said he was in a poker game in the park's clubhouse till two in the morning. He then went home to sleep off the beer he drank because he had to mow grass at eight the next morning. Calvin then asked why the request for an alibi if he was certain the death was a suicide. The detective said it was just a routine question he was required to ask. The answer seemed to satisfy Calvin.

The detective had no more questions. He told them that the medical examiner would release the body for burial the next day.

Billy called their Aunt Irene to find out if there was a family plot available. She said there wasn't for that side of the relation. The three brothers agreed to have the body cremated. Billy volunteered to spread the ashes in the national forest when they were available. Calvin said he wouldn't care if he threw them in the dumpster. The arrangements were made for the crematorium to pick up the body at the morgue and to let Billy know when the ashes were ready to be picked up.

Three days later Billy made the trip back to Zephyrhills alone. The crematorium had placed his father's ashes in a Styrofoam take home box just like his adoptive mother's. Billy thought they could have used a more dignified container but the Styrofoam box served the purpose. Ashes to ashes and dust to dust, but the container would be in the environment for centuries.

He cut over through the Ocala National Forest on his way back home and spread his father's ashes in the forest along a secluded stretch of Route 19. He deposited the Styrofoam box in a roadside trash receptacle.

Chapter 15

Early June 2009 – Ocala

Brantley was reading his Bible and preparing his material for the upcoming revivals when his phone rang. "Hello, Reverend Billy Brantley speaking."

"Reverend, this is Harvey Skaggs from Zephyrhills. I am the owner of the Wood Dale Mobile Home Park where your late father rented a double wide. I need you to come down here as soon as you can to move your father's things out. The place is being leased again in two weeks. I need at least a week to clean it up."

"Mr. Skaggs, my brothers and I will be down in about three days to do as you wish."

"Thank you reverend, I appreciate your prompt action."

The disposition of their father's house and possessions had not crossed Brantley's mind. He called Calvin to see if he wanted to make the trip back to the house. Calvin said he had taken everything he wanted when he left in May. He said the rest of the stuff could be given to Goodwill or hauled to the landfill. Besides that he couldn't get away from his job at the RV park.

The call to Franklin produced a more congenial response. Franklin said he could use a few items for his rental house, as it looked quite empty at the moment. He said he would rent a small U-haul truck and pick Billy up on the way. Franklin arrived late that night at Billy's house in Ocala. He had left Jacksonville right after his shift ended at the sheriff's office.

Billy had some business to do down in Orlando after taking care of their father's possessions so he said he would follow Franklin in his own truck. The next morning they made the short drive to Zephyrhills. Billy helped Franklin load a dinette set, a leather recliner that was in amazingly good shape, and a few smaller chairs and tables into the U-haul. He was thinking about taking along the outdoor BBQ grill but decided it was too badly damaged. While Franklin was packing up some much needed dishes, pots and pans, and silverware, Billy rummaged through the closets. On the top shelf of his father's bedroom he found a box of old photographs. Billy recognized his mother in a few of the photos as his Aunt Irene had showed him pictures of his mother last month. One was a photo of his mother and her Uncle James posing under a live oak tree. "Hey Frankie, come here and look at this."

Franklin came into the bedroom and Billy handed him the picture. "I'll be darned, that is our mother and father together. Now we know where we get our good looks. Uncle James wasn't too bad looking in his younger days."

A Goodwill truck pulled up out front and tooted the horn. Billy had made arrangements for them to pick up the remainder of the items in the house. While they were emptying the house and the storage shed, Billy continued rummaging through the closets and bedroom dresser. In the top drawer of the dresser he came across a small thirty-eight special snub nose revolver and a box of ammunition. He thought about telling Franklin but then put it in the box with the old photos. At least he had something he could consider an inheritance from his father.

With the house cleaned out to the landlord's satisfaction Franklin left to head back to Jacksonville. The landlord handed Billy a check for five hundred dollars that had been his father's rental deposit in case of damages to the house. Billy thanked him for his honesty as the landlord could have just kept the deposit and Billy would have been none the wiser.

Billy headed to Orlando to meet with a person an acquaintance in Ocala told him about. He was described as a shady character but did excellent work and was discreet. The landlord's check would come in handy.

Following his business in Orlando he arrived at the airport with an hour to spare before boarding his flight to Belize. He had further business to attend to in the Central American country.

****

The next year was mainly uneventful for the three brothers. Calvin was enjoying his stay and job at the RV park. He even settled into a half-decent social life. He attended a few of Billy's revivals when they were in a nearby town.

Franklin settled into his new rental house. His job on the Jacksonville Sheriff's Bomb Squad was going extremely well as was his romance with the blond realtor.

Billy's revival schedule was filling up for the coming year. He even had one scheduled as far out as the following July in Pensacola. Though things were going well for Billy he often thought about his stepbrother Calvin's strange behavior when his stepbrother attended his revivals. Perhaps Calvin would prove to be useful in his future plans.

PART THREE

Chapter 16

Friday morning, July 16, 2010, Chattanooga

The police cruiser arrived twenty minutes after Becky Wilcox's scream. One of her coworkers had to call 911 as her hands were shaking too much to manipulate her cell phone. A second patrol car arrived three minutes later followed by a detective's unmarked blue Ford sedan.

A uniformed policeman asked Becky to move her vehicle to make room for the coroner's van. She was no longer shaking but handed the keys that were still clutched in her hand to the officer saying she was still too upset to drive. The officer moved the Hyundai and then proceeded to cordon off the area with yellow police tape.

Detective Barry Langford asked Becky if she was the person who found the body.

"Yes, sir, I am", she replied. "I just pulled into the lot and parked in my usual space at the end of the lot down here. I am afraid of tourists dinging my doors if I park closer to the entrance. I got out of my car and as soon as I closed my door I saw the body. It was horrible."

Langford asked, "Did you or anybody touch or move the body or move anything on it?"

"No, sir. Are you kidding? I was too petrified to move. All I could do was stand there and scream. Jimmy over there helped steady me and we walked back away from the body, then he called 911."

"What time did you leave work yesterday?"

"I left shortly after two."

"Thank you, Ms. Wilcox. That will be all for now. Please move back near the building entrance with the rest of your coworkers."

Langford questioned the rest of the employees as a group. Everyone had left at about the same time the previous day and nothing out of the ordinary had occurred. No one saw a body.

"Then there is a different crew that works until closing time at eight?"

A heavyset woman in a khaki and white Ruby Falls uniform spoke, "Yes there is a different afternoon to eight crew. I am the morning manager, Dolores Glass."

"Ms. Glass, would you inform the afternoon manager that I will be back at four o'clock to talk to the other employees?"

"Yes, sir, I will."

The medical examiner and a crime scene technician arrived and proceeded to process the body and surrounding area. The brush around the back side of the parking lot was searched for anything that could relate to the crime. The only thing that was found was the usual tourist litter.

The note and the rock were handled with gloved hands and put into plastic evidence bags. Using the victim's body temperature and degree of rigor mortis the medical examiner determined the time of death to be between 10P.M. and midnight. The body was approaching full rigor. Full rigor occurs approximately twelve hours after death. Thus with the correlation of the body temperature and degree of rigor he determined the time of death to be between nine and eleven hours ago. It was now 9am. He surmised that the wounds in the chest were made after the victim had died. The small amount of blood around the wounds indicated that the heart had already stopped beating. The wounds were of uniform depth and made with a very sharp instrument, possibly from a utility knife with the blade only partially extended. With the absence of any other physical wounds that could cause death the examiner suspected either asphyxiation or drug overdose. The exact cause of death would have to be determined at the autopsy.

Tourists had started to arrive and were being delayed on the access road. Some were leaving their cars and hiking up through the grounds to see what all the ado was about.

Detective Langford saw the news van with satellite dish arrive. The Channel 17 reporter approached him and he told her as cordially as he could that there would be no interviews at this time. A statement would be made downtown in the police station's media room after the crime scene was cleared. They did, however, manage to film the body bag being loaded into the medical examiners van.

One of the co-reporters came running up and said she found the person that discovered the body. The camera crew then headed to the Ruby Falls entrance where Becky Wilcox was still standing. Becky was excited that she would be on the news being interviewed about the gruesome crime.

The Same Morning

Hank was sitting under the Bounder's awning enjoying the morning air when he called Gerry Baker, his old partner back at the Kenner police station. Baker had to be paged and there was a two minute wait before he answered his phone. "Detective Gerry Baker, anyone still there?"

"Hey you old fart how are you doing?"

"Hey, Hank, look who's calling who an old fart. I'm not the one who packed it in and retired."

"That's because you didn't save your money. You blew it all on women and booze. Now you're stuck with working till you drop."

"Yeah, well . . . but I had a hell of a good time."

"Gerry, all kidding aside, I wonder if you could do me a favor."

"Sure, Hank, what is it."

"I have a Florida tag number that I need you to run and see if you can come up with the owner's name and address."

"What in hell are you into, Hank? You're retired."

"I just stumbled into something in our travels and it looks like it might be a serial murder situation."

"Hank, be careful sticking your nose into something like that. You spent I don't know how many years on the force dodging all kinds of crap without a scratch. It would be a shame to hear that you were bumped off in your first year of retirement. You and Helen be careful. You packing?"

"No, Gerry, I am not packing, and we are taking everything we find to the local police."

"OK, Hank, give me that tag number and I'll call you back in ten with the information."

"Thanks, Gerry, I really appreciate your concern, and we'll keep a low profile."

Hank gave his old partner the Florida tag number and his cell phone number.

"Hey, Gerry, before I forget, how's your new partner working out?"

"She's a hell of a lot better to look at than you, Hank. Actually she's doing quite well. Smart gal, too, and in shape. Sometimes it's a chore for these old bones to keep up with her."

"Sounds like you better start hitting the gym instead of Lucky's Lounge."

"Hank I'm afraid it's too late to make any difference. One session in the gym and Maxine will be looking for a new partner."

"OK, Gerry, don't forget to call back with that tag info if you're not too out of breath."

"Will do, smart ass. Bye."

Helen had the TV on as she was sitting at the dinette working on the morning paper's crossword puzzle. She was just filling in the answer to a four letter word that means "to kill" when a news bulletin aired.

"A body has been found in the Ruby Falls parking lot at eight this morning by an arriving employee. We will take you now to reporter, Mitzi Taylor, live at the scene."

"This is Mitzi Taylor live at the scene in the Ruby Falls parking lot where a man's body was found by a female employee when she arrived at work just before eight this morning. Detectives at the scene gave no immediate comment, stating a press conference will be held at the downtown station after the crime scene is cleared.

However, we were able to locate the employee that discovered the body. Standing here with me is Becky Wilcox, and she has a gruesome tale to tell. Becky, how did you find the body?"

"I had just stepped out of my parked car and closed the door when a man's body caught my eye just off the edge of the parking lot. When I saw it all I could do was scream. It was so horrible."

"Becky, what was so horrible that made you scream?"

"The dead guy's shirt was wide open and it looked like a big 'X' was cut into his chest. Right above the 'X' was a yellow post-it type note. It was partially stuck under a rock that was right under the guy's chin."

"Did you see if anything was written on the note?"

"There was something written there but I was too upset to make it out. Jimmy Bressler, my co-worker who called 911, said he saw what was on it."

"And what did Jimmy see?"

"He said it was a bible quote, LEV 20:13, and under that it said, 'Fire and brimstone next.'"

"Thank you, Becky!"

The camera panned off Becky and back to Mitzy Taylor.

"The police still do not know or are withholding the identity of the victim. We should learn more at the downtown news conference later this morning."

Helen shouted, "Hank, Hank, where are you?"

Hank, entering their motor home, answered, "What is it? I was on the phone with Gerry."

"You just missed the news bulletin. There's been another murder. Looks like our killer struck again. Same note only this time he added something. He wrote 'Fire and Brimstone Next' under the bible verse."

"Hmm, sounds like he is planning something bigger for the next victim. Where did they find the body?"

"At the Ruby Falls parking lot just before eight this morning. The police wouldn't give any information on the victim. Maybe they are trying to locate next of kin."

"I doubt that is the way he wanted to see Ruby Falls."

Fifteen minutes later Hank's cell phone rang. He opted for a plain ordinary ring on his cell rather than some crazy musical rendition of the William Tell Overture. He was always annoyed when he heard other peoples cells go off. Especially when his old partner's phone erupted with the Camptown Races. "Hey, Gerry, what have you got?"

"I have that tag info for you, Hank. The truck is registered to a Calvin Bixler from Zephyrhills, Florida. Number eighteen Boston Avenue."

"Thanks, Gerry, I'll have to pass that along to the local police up here in Chattanooga. It looks like our killer struck again last night."

"Hank, take my advice and stay out of it. Let the locals handle it."

"Yeah, Gerry, I'm passing what I have on to the locals but this thing is multi-state for sure now and I think the FBI will get wind of it soon."

"That's too bad, Hank, They'll fuck it up for sure."

"We never did think too highly of them did we, Gerry. OK, thanks for the rundown on that tag. I'll be in touch."

"Hank, please take my advice. Talk to you later."

"Was that Gerry on the phone again?" Helen asked.

"Yeah, that was Gerry. I had him run the tag number of that guy's F-250. It's registered to a Calvin Bixler from Zephyrhills down in Florida."

"He may be a relative to Reverend Brantley. They do have a close resemblance to each other. Could be cousins. They have different surnames."

"I'm gonna give Bill Anspach a call. He worked for a big newspaper in Indy and I bet he knows someone who can research the news for the central Florida area for anything on the preacher and Mr. Bixler."

"Aren't you going to contact the Chattanooga police about the serial killer situation?"

"I guess I should call them first. Only thing is they will have to contact the Feds because it does cross a few state lines."

"Hank, I know how you feel about the FBI, but they have the resources to deal with this. Chattanooga doesn't."

"OK, I'll give the police a call. I just hope it won't be like talking to a wall. While I'm calling them why don't you call Journey Church to see if the preacher is still there. And try to get his cell phone number if they have it."

Hank found the Chattanooga Police Department's phone number on the City of Chattanooga Web site. He went back outside and sat at the picnic table and dialed. After getting past the dispatcher he managed to talk to the desk sergeant. Hank asked to talk to the detective in charge of the Ruby Falls investigation but was told he was not available. He explained who he was and gave the sergeant all the information about the two previous murders and the possible involvement of Reverend Brantley. The sergeant asked for Hank's phone number and said he would pass the information on to detective Langford when he got out of the news conference.

Helen leaned out the door of the Bounder. "Hank, I just talked to Reverend Stiles and he said Reverend Brantley pulled out at about eight-thirty this morning. He told Reverend Stiles he had to go up to the Tri-Cities area for another revival tomorrow evening. He didn't say what church."

"Did he have the preacher's phone number?"

"Yes, he did. I have it written down."

Hank jogged up to the end of their row of RV sites to see if Calvin Bixler's rig was still there. The trailer was there, but his truck was gone. He then walked the short distance to the park office and asked the clerk if she saw what time Bixler left. She said she opened the office at eight and didn't see him pass by. He must have left quite early.

Chapter 17

Friday morning, July 16, 2010 – Chattanooga

Hank was walking back from the campground office trying to work out the next plan of action. What he wanted was to be on the road towards the upstate Tri-Cities area. He knew he would be just spinning his wheels chasing the preacher around the country, one step behind him, if he didn't obtain background knowledge on the man.

He got back to his picnic table command center and dialed Bill Anspach. Jenny answered the phone, "Hello, Jenny, this is Hank Moran. Is Bill around?"

"He walked the trash up to the dumpster. He's coming back down the road now. What's happening, Hank?"

"Oh, just another murder here in Chattanooga. I wanted to ask Bill a favor."

"Really! Another murder? That will give him something for his next article. Oh maybe I shouldn't have said anything. It's best if he tells you. Here he is now. Bill, it's Hank on the phone."

Jenny handed the phone to Bill.

"Hello, Hank! What's happening?"

"Bill, there has been another murder by the Leviticus killer here in Chattanooga. I wanted to ask a favor of you."

"Sure, Hank. What do you need?"

"I know you still have connections back at the Indianapolis Star and I was wondering if anyone on the staff could do some research and perform a background check on Reverend Brantley. I just discovered that he has a possible relative by the name of Calvin Bixler from Zephyrhills tagging along in another rig."

"Hank, I'm way ahead of you on the preacher. I did some checking on him for my weekly column. Remember, I told you the paper wanted me to do a weekly piece about interesting places we see and interesting people we meet? Well, the preacher is one of the interesting people. The column starts in this Sunday's edition and mentions the preacher and the first two murders."

"Are Helen and I also two of the interesting people?"

"Well, you are, but I didn't mention your names. Only that you are a retired Louisiana homicide detective and his wife, traveling in your motor home, investigating the murders."

"Bill, thanks for not revealing our names. What did you learn about the preacher?"

"Well, he is a legitimate preacher with a college degree. Drifted around from church to church for a number of years as an assistant minister before he found his own gigs. His last one was in Mt. Dora where they fired him because he was turning more radical by the month. The attendance was dropping and they decided to open the church to all who are interested, including gays. They figured this would be at great odds with Brantley's anti-gay sermons so they let him go."

"Seems like there is a motive building with his anti-gay themes. When did he begin on the revival circuit?"

"That is still unclear. Somehow he went from a near penniless preacher living in a small apartment above a garage to roaming the country in a big, expensive rig. That's all I could gather for now. It's still a work in progress. Tell me about this new murder. I might have time to add it to my first column."

Hank told Bill about the latest murder and the additional line to the note left on the victim. He had not heard if the victim was gay. He told Bill to include the name Calvin Bixler from Zephyrhills in his research and to call as soon as he learned more details.

Hank had just sat down in the Bounder to enjoy the BLT sandwich Helen had prepared for him when his cell phone rang again. "Hello, Hank Moran here."

"Mr. Moran, this is detective Barry Langford from the Chattanooga Police Department. Our desk sergeant mentioned that you had called about the Ruby Falls case, and I'd like a few words with you. Are you available to come down to the station?"

"Actually, no, I can't. We are in the process of breaking camp here to head up to the Tri-Cities area. If you hurry you can catch us up here at the KOA in Cleveland or talk over the phone. And actually, I told the desk sergeant everything I know."

"That's fine, Mr. Moran, but I would like to talk to you personally. There may be something that you might have forgotten to mention. I can be there in twenty minutes if you can wait."

"OK. If you insist, we'll be here, detective. Site number thirty-one."

Detective Langford showed up twenty-five minutes later. He had gotten tied up in traffic trying to get out of Chattanooga. Hank was waiting for him at the picnic table.

Double checking the site number Langford walked up to the picnic table.

"Mr. Moran?"

"You found me, detective."

"Looks like you're almost ready to pull out."

"Disconnect the power and hook up the Honda and we're gone. What can I do for you?"

"Mr. Moran, the desk sergeant mentioned two other victims of similar crimes in two other towns. What makes you think we have a serial situation going on?"

"Same type of note with the same bible verse left on the victim. Bodies dumped in a similar manner, and victims were gay men. At least the first two were, and I'll bet you find your vic was also."

"You are a recently retired detective from Kenner?

"Yes, I am."

"How did you find out about the first murder in Gulf Breeze?

"We were camping down in Biloxi and I read about it in the newspaper. The article mentioned the post-it note with the bible verse. There was a preacher staying at the same campground with the same bible verse on his rig. Our next door neighbor mentioned that he and his wife had attended the preacher's tent revival down in Gulf Breeze. The preacher fit the description also."

"What happened next? What about the murder in Biloxi?"

"Well, detective, we heard about that one on a TV news bulletin. I then talked to the Harrison County Sheriff's deputy in charge of the investigation and informed him of the similar murder in Gulf Breeze. At that point there were too many coincidences so we followed the preacher up here."

"Where is this preacher now?"

"I am sorry to say he has left the area and is heading up to the Tri-Cities area. Just where, I don't know yet. We are planning to motor up there to see if we can track him down. I think he—or they—are planning something bigger for the next victim based on the addition of the line, 'Fire and brimstone next,' to the note. The first two notes just had the bible verse."

"Do you happen to have this Reverend Brantley's phone number?"

"Yes, my wife, Helen, has it. I'll get it."

Hank came back out of the Bounder with the number and gave it to the detective. "We were going to call him when we got up to the Tri-Cities to find out where his revival is tomorrow night."

"Mr. Moran, where were you between nine and midnight last night?"

"Hank smiled and said, "I thought you would never get around to asking that. I would have asked the same question. We were at the preacher's revival meeting until after nine. Then I drove my wife back to the coach to watch for Brantley's buddy while I drove back to the church to stake out the preacher's trailer. He came home at about 11:30. I then drove back to the KOA and Brantley's buddy pulled into the campground just ahead of me.

Langford grinned and slowly shook his head. "I see. Who is this buddy you mentioned?"

"He seems to be an acquaintance of the preacher's. He has a good likeness to the preacher so we thought he might be a relative. He was at the revival also. Both he and the preacher could be the person in the composite sketch of the Biloxi suspect that Deputy Reed emailed to me."

"See, this is something you didn't mention. Could I see that sketch?"

"Sure." Hank called into the motor home for Helen to bring out the police sketch from Deputy Reed. Helen was busy preparing the inside of the Bounder for travel making sure all loose items were off the counters and stowed and whatever else had to be tied down. She handed the sketch out to Hank.

Detective Langford looked at the sketch and asked if he could keep it. He said he would like to show it to a potential witness.

Hank said, "Sure, you can have it if it will help you with the investigation. However, I think the killer is already out of the area and headed to the Tri-Cities area. I would advise you to contact detective LaFollette from Gulf Breeze and Deputy Reed from the Harrison County Sheriff's Office for additional information. I am sure they would be very interested in your case as well. They might have additional findings in their cases that could help you."

"Thank you for the information, Mr. Moran. I'll let you get on your way. Here is my card if you think of anything else. I have your number in case I want to talk to you again. Oh, and be very careful with your investigation. I realize you were the only one to tie these crimes together, but things could get very dangerous for you and your wife. I'd hate to hear you had a very brief retirement, if you catch my drift."

"My friends keep telling me the same thing, but until this thing is solved I feel I need to stay on top of it. Will you be calling in the Feds on the case?"

"Not at this time. In fact if anything else happens up-state, like you think it might, the local police or the Tennessee State Police would handle it as long as it is within our borders."

"Well, good luck in your investigation, Detective Langford."

"Thank you, take care, Mr. Moran."

Ten minutes earlier inside the Bounder

Helen punched in Brantley's number on her cell phone and he answered on the fourth ring.

"Hello, Reverend Billy Brantley speaking."

"Reverend Brantley, this is Clara Blakely from down in Cleveland, I was just talking with Mrs. Stiles at the Journey Church and she said you were a wonderful minister and held an outstanding revival meeting there. Unfortunately I was out of town and missed it. She said you had another revival up in the Tri-Cities area and my husband and I would so much like to attend. Could you tell me the name of the church? We can hop in our motor home and make a weekend trip out of it."

"Sure, come on up. The revival is at the Mountain Missionary Church just outside of Walkertown on Route 93."

"Are there any RV parks close by where we could stay?"

"I'll be camping at the Cedar Springs RV Park near Fall Branch. They might still have a site available."

"Thank you very much, reverend, you are so dear. We'll see you tomorrow night."

"Thanks for calling, Mrs. Blakely. Goodbye."

Helen saw the Chattanooga detective leave and she opened the door, "Come on, Hank, hook up the Honda, we have to go. I know where the preacher is going and I already made reservations at a campground."

Helen was taking in the beautiful countryside on the way to the Tri-Cities. As they passed several fields with grazing cattle Helen remarked, "Hank, did you notice that all those grazing cattle were facing in the same direction?"

"Yeah, that's quite common. They are just following the leader of the herd. It reminds me of the good Reverend Brantley and his congregation. Brantley is the leader of the herd and there is no one in the congregation capable of a free thought to turn in another direction."

The Friday afternoon traffic on Interstate 40 through Knoxville was at a crawl. The Morans finally reached the campground in the Tri-Cities area near Baileyton at five o'clock. The Tri-Cities is a region in extreme northeast Tennessee consisting of the three major cities of Kingsport, Johnson City, and Bristol, plus the surrounding area.

While they were setting up the camp and extending the slides Hank's cell phone rang. Bill Anspach was on the line.

"Hank, I have some more news on the preacher for you. My researcher, Mary Sue, called the church in Mt. Dora and they said the preacher has a twin brother. It's kind of a long story so hang in there."

"I'm all ears, Bill. Don't keep me in suspense."

"Well, a lot of the preachers in the area know each other and gossip like a bunch of old women. It seems our dear reverend was adopted and his adoptive mother died a little over a year ago and left him quite a bit of money. While on her deathbed his mother told him he was adopted and that he has a twin brother from whom he was separated. The brother was adopted by a couple named Whitehead, and of course he was adopted by the Brantleys."

"So they are twin brothers with different last names."

"That's right, but it gets better. The preacher buys a new rig and he and his brother head down to central Florida to look up their long lost relatives. They find out their mother's name was Nancy Bixler who died while giving birth to them at the age of sixteen. Their father was actually their mother's uncle so the twins' father is also their great uncle. Their father also fathered another son a few years later and his name is Calvin Bixler. He is their stepbrother and/or cousin."

"Bill, that sounds like enough to screw up a person's head."

"There's more. The grandfather won the lottery and put a small fortune in trust for the twins if they should happen to show up and claim it within ten years. He felt guilty because he couldn't afford to raise the boys and had them put up for adoption. Well, they both claimed over seven-hundred grand with a year to spare."

"So, that explains the preacher's sudden wealth. What does his twin brother do for a living?"

"His name is Franklin Whitehead and works on the bomb squad in Jacksonville. Oh, and they also mentioned that the stepbrother, Calvin, suffers from some mental disorder called DID. It's a multiple personality type thing."

"Well, Bill, we got an overzealous preacher who has a twin that works on a bomb squad, and a crazy stepbrother. Sounds like quite a cast of characters. And the thing is all three of them would look like the composite police sketch of the killer."

"Hank, I'll leave it up to you to figure that all out. In the meantime I have plenty to write about in my column."

"It's beginning to sound like you could turn it into a full-length novel."

"Can I use your and Helen's names?"

"Hell no. Fake them."

"Well, that's all I have for now. I told Mary Sue she could take a break and get back to her regular work. See you later, Hank."

"So long, Bill. Thanks."

Chapter 18

Saturday Evening, July 17, 2010

The Morans arrived at the Mountain Missionary Church in Walkertown just as the tent revival festivities were starting. This time they brought their own comfortable lawn chairs figuring there would be SRO for late arrivals. As they made their way to the tent they made it a point to check the parking lot for Calvin Bixler's truck. They couldn't spot it. They found a place for their chairs under the tent near the edge of the regular seating.

A bluegrass band was playing gospel music when they arrived. They were quite good and Hank told Helen that he would rather listen to them all night instead of Brantley.

Brantley was at his usual vociferous best. The Morans perused the audience but could not spot Calvin. Helen said, "Reverend Brantley is a very good inspirational speaker."

"I agree." Hank replied. "But, he could also be a cold blooded killer. I think it is time we have a talk with Brantley. Let's try to get him alone after the services."

Brantley socialized for thirty minutes after the revival and then headed for his truck. Hank and Helen were waiting for him. Brantley saw them as he approached and nodded. "Good evening, folks."

Hank said, "Reverend, can we have a word with you?"

"You two look familiar," Brantley said. "I think I saw you at the revival down in Cleveland."

"Yes, you did. We enjoyed the program. I am Hank Moran and this is my wife, Helen.

"Glad to meet you both. What can I do for you?"

"Reverend, are you aware there has been a series of murders of homosexual men in the same towns as your last three revivals? Also, the murders took place either the same night or the next day after your revivals."

"Mr. Moran, I was not aware of that. I really don't read the papers or watch much television. I do try to catch the Sunday TV services when I get the chance."

"I see, reverend. I know you left town the next day after your revivals, so maybe you weren't aware of the murders. By the way, where is your brother, Calvin, tonight? We saw him at your last revival."

"Calvin said he had to go back to his home in Florida after the Cleveland revival. He had to get back to his job at the campground where he is staying."

Helen asked, "Was Calvin with you for the Pensacola revival?"

"No, he wasn't. He only attended a couple of them"

"How about the Biloxi revival?"

"Yes, he was at the Biloxi revival. Why all the questions about my stepbrother and how do you know his name? Are you working with the police?"

Hank answered, "We are just concerned citizens who noticed the correlation between your revivals and the murders. We have given the local police what information we have gathered. We obtained Calvin's name through his truck tag. We think Calvin may know something about the murders."

"What makes you think he would know about the murders?"

"Reverend, we obtained a copy of the composite police sketch of the suspect in the Biloxi slaying. The sketch has a striking resemblance to both you and your stepbrother. A note was placed on each victim with the same bible verse you have on the side of your camper."

"Are you accusing my brother or me of murder, Mr. Moran?

"Not at this point, reverend. We have more investigating to do. The murderer could be someone who is following you around and taking your sermons about the demise of gays literally. I would be very careful, reverend. That person would be mentally unstable and might just kill the messenger."

"Thanks for the warning, Mr. Moran. I'll keep that in mind."

"Where is your next revival?" Helen asked.

"I will be going to Roanoke, Virginia. The revival is in ten days. I plan to visit a few churches here in the area before I leave. Anything else, Mrs. Moran, or should I call you Mrs. Blakely?"

Helen just smiled and said, "Mrs. Moran will do."

The Morans thanked the reverend and said it was nice talking with him. Brantley said he wished he could say the same.

As the Morans were driving back to the campground Hank said, "Well, I think that conversation pushed a few of the preacher's buttons."

"He may panic and leave the area," Helen replied.

"I don't think so. I have a feeling he has something planned over the next week."

"Do you mean something related to the 'Fire and brimstone next' part of the note?"

"Exactly, Helen."

Dade City Florida, 1:00 A.M.

Calvin stopped at the gate for the Cook Brothers Construction Company. He exited his truck and softly called out for Ripper. "Come here, boy, remember me?" The large guard dog suddenly appeared on the other side of the fence and let out a soft "ruff."

Then his tail wagged as he recognized Calvin after more than a year. Calvin stuck his fingers through the fence and received a friendly lick. "Good boy."

Calvin couldn't believe they still had the same old combination lock on the gate. He slipped through the gate and with a duffel bag and bolt cutters in his hands and made his way to the explosives shed. Ripper followed playfully at his side. The bolt cutters made short work of the padlock. He found everything he needed, closed the door, and headed back to his truck. He rewarded Ripper with two large dog biscuits and a new rawhide chew.

He hung the lock in the hasp and was on his way.

Sunday, July 18th, 2010 – Indianapolis

Bill Anspach's column, "On the Road with Bill and Jenny," ran in the travel section of the Sunday *Star*. The column gave mainly sightseeing information about the Biloxi and Chattanooga areas. Near the end of the column, however, Bill mentioned the mysterious preacher they had met and his possible connection to a series of murders of gay men in the cities of Gulf Breeze, Biloxi, and Chattanooga. He mentioned the notes left on the bodies and printed the Leviticus 20:13 bible verse in its entirety. He mentioned that a recently retired Louisiana homicide detective and his wife were on the trail of the Leviticus killer. As promised, he didn't include the names of the preacher or the Morans.

Agent Ben Horton was reading the Sunday *Star* with his feet propped up on his desk at the FBI's Indianapolis branch office on Pennsylvania Street. It was his Sunday to man the office phones and emails on the slight chance Indy received some urgent orders from headquarters. He was reading Bill's column and daydreaming about buying a motor home when he came across the part about the reverend and the murders. His feet came off the desk and the phone was in his hand in two seconds dialing the FBI branch office coordinator in Washington.

The phone in Washington was answered by Charlie Simpson trying to stifle a yawn.

"Charlie, this is Ben Horton in Indy. I was just reading a travel column in the *Indy Star* and the writer, a Bill Anspach, mentioned a series of slayings of gay men in three southern states. The same message was placed on all three victims. And get this: a vacationing retired detective is trying to track down the killer. Do you have anything on this?"

"I haven't, but one of the other coordinators might. Let me check the computer, and I'll get right back with you. In the meantime get in touch with this Bill Anspach and find out all he knows. We need the names of the people involved and a way to contact them."

Agent Horton saw that Bill had printed his email address at the end of his column. Horton fired off an email asking Bill to call the Indianapolis FBI Office as soon as possible. As he pushed send his office phone rang. It was Simpson at headquarters calling back.

"Ben, this is Charlie. We have no information on anything having to do with the serial murder situation you called about. When you have gathered all the information on the principals involved pass it on to Chris Emory in Knoxville. If the last slaying occurred in Chattanooga his office should handle it."

"Do you think Emory can handle it?"

"I'm sure he can. He was just young and a little hasty in New Orleans when he bungled that bank robbery investigation. He has matured in the last five years. Just forward everything to him. In the meantime I'll call and tell him to begin contacting the local police in each of the cities involved."

"OK, Charlie, will do."

Nashville, Tennessee

Bill Anspach was writing his next column about the Nashville area and the Grand Ole Opry when his email account chimed; he saved his work on the word processor and checked his email. The new message was from an Agent Horton from the FBI's Indy Office urging Bill to call the number given as soon as possible. Bill guessed it had to be about his Sunday column. Thinking it might be someone pretending to be an agent, he checked the FBI Web site for the phone number of the Indy office. The numbers matched.

Bill reluctantly dialed the number and agent Horton answered.

"Agent Horton, this is Bill Anspach from the *Star*. I am responding to your email request to give you a call. What's up?"

Mr. Anspach, the Bureau is extremely interested in your story about the reverend and the gay men who were murdered. First of all I need to ask you: is the story a work of fiction or it is fact?

"I assure you the story is real, Agent Horton."

"That being said, Mr. Anspach, I would like the names of the people involved plus phone numbers where they can be reached. This is now an official FBI investigation, and your cooperation is required."

"I see. I am sure the paper would like me to cooperate. I will help you any way I can."

Bill proceeded to relate the entire story about the preacher and the Morans' involvement in trying to solve the murders. He was actually glad that the FBI was now involved. He was fearful for the Morans' safety as they inched closer to the killer.

"Mr. Anspach, you said the retired detective's name was Hank Moran from Kenner, Louisiana?"

"That's right. From your tone you sound like you might know him."

"I think the Bureau has had some experience in the past with Detective Moran. Thank you for your cooperation, Mr. Anspach. The Bureau appreciates it."

When Bill hung up with Agent Horton he immediately called Hank and informed him of the FBI's interest in the murders. He told Hank to be expecting a call from them as he had no choice but to give them Hank's number. Hank assured Bill that it was OK that he had given out his phone number.

After the call from Bill Anspach Agent Horton went over his notes then called agent Chris Emory from the Knoxville office. Emory answered his cell phone from his bass boat on Douglass Lake east of Knoxville.

"Chris, this is Ben Horton from the Indy office. Simpson up in headquarters wanted me to call you with some data on the homo slayings."

"Yeah, Ben, you guys sure know how to ruin a guy's Sunday. A six pound largemouth just got off the hook when I reached for my phone."

"Sorry for your loss, Chris, but I have a little tidbit you might find interesting. Did Charlie mention there was a retired homicide detective involved with the case?"

"Yeah, he did. So what?

"The retiree is your old buddy from down in Kenner, Hank Moran."

"You've got to be shitting me."

"'Fraid not. Call me when you get to the office and I'll fill you in on all the details."

"I won't make it to the office today. It will be first thing in the morning."

"OK. Take care, Chris. I hope you land that six pounder. Talk to you in the morning."

Hank and Agent Emory had crossed paths in New Orleans in 2005 in the aftermath of Hurricane Katrina. An enterprising pair of bank robbers had stolen an NOPD police car and uniforms and robbed a bank in Kenner, Louisiana. Hank was the lead detective assigned to the case. The FBI investigated and arrested two NOPD policemen. Hank cleared the officers and arrested the actual bank robbers. Agent Emory was the lead FBI investigator and was subsequently reassigned to the Knoxville field office. He considered it punishment for botching the investigation and arresting the wrong suspects. He had to make a formal apology to the NOPD. Hank received the Detective of the Year award from Kenner and a citation from the NOPD.

Monday July 19th, 2010 — Knoxville

Agent Emory arrived at the FBI field office on Dowell Springs Boulevard early on Monday morning. He called Agent Horton in Indy and received all the pertinent information on the case. He then phoned the Chattanooga Police Department to talk with the detective in charge of the latest slaying. Arrangements were made to meet with Detective Langford at one that afternoon. He had to leave Knoxville by ten-thirty in order to make the meeting in

Chattanooga. He still had time to call the Gulf Breeze police and the Harrison County Mississippi Sheriff's Office.

Detective LaFollette of The Gulf breeze police had made some progress in his investigation. He had learned of the other two murders from Detective Langford of Chattanooga. With the help of a police sketch artist, the waitress, Beth McDaniels, from the Hampton Inn on Pensacola Beach, was able to put together a portrait of the man who had drinks with the victim the night of the murder. After showing her pictures of various trucks they were able to determine that the truck the victim and suspect drove away in was a black late model Ford F-250 diesel. LaFollette said he would email the portrait and a copy of the note left on the body to Agent Emory. Emory requested that a copy of the entire investigation file including the coroner's report be overnighted to him.

Next he talked to Deputy Reed from the Harrison County Sheriff's Office. Deputy Reed's investigation had come to a standstill. The only viable information he had was the composite sketch of the suspect who was drinking with the victim. He promised to email the sketch along with a copy of the note left on the body to Agent Emory. Once again Emory requested that a copy of the entire file be overnighted to him.

Emory was saving the call to Moran for last. He needed time to decide just how he wanted to handle the retired detective. Besides he wanted to get entirely familiar with the murders before meeting with Moran. This time he wanted to keep one step ahead of the detective with no screw ups.

Agent Emory arrived in Chattanooga right on time for the one o'clock meeting with Detective Langford. They met in the small conference room right behind the Chief's office. The room was Spartan with a six-foot long scarred wood top table and steel framed chairs with minimal padding. Several empty soda cans and an empty pizza box were left on the middle of the table.

Langford apologized for the mess stating the room was also used as the department's lunch room. Emory got right down to business.

"Detective Langford, I need everything you have on the murder of the victim that was found at Ruby Falls last Friday morning. That includes a copy of your file to date. I'll also need to see the note that was left on the victim. Why don't we start with you telling me what you have?"

"Well, Agent Emory, the victim's name is Anthony Edwards. He was last seen Thursday evening at Images Night Club here in Chattanooga. The night club is a well known gay establishment. We have established from the victim's friends that he was indeed gay. A witness stated that he thought he saw the victim sitting with another guy in a large black pickup truck. It appeared that the victim was sleeping with his head against the door jamb on the passenger side of the truck. But he could not positively identify the person as the victim. The witness entered the club as the truck was leaving."

"Was anybody able to remember the guy with the truck?"

"The bartender said there was a guy he never saw before who sat at the bar. He was just sitting, drinking, and smiling while watching the dance floor. He paid his tab and left right before the victim. Unfortunately, he paid cash for the tab."

"Was that the last anyone saw the victim?"

"Either the bartender or the witness in the parking lot was the last that we know of to date."

"OK, detective, let's move on to the actual murder. What was the cause of death?"

"The coroner's report will be in your copy of my file. The actual cause of death was suffocation but it appeared that the victim was injected with a dose of medetomidine which is an immobilizing drug vets and zoos use to immobilize large animals. The victim could have been shot with a tranquilizer dart gun or injected directly with a syringe. The injection was in the left shoulder. From the trauma around the injection point the coroner is leaning toward a dart gun. There were traces of an adhesive on the victim's neck. It was the same type adhesive that is used on duct tape. We figured the killer immobilized the victim and then suffocated him by sealing a plastic bag over his head."

"Were there any other signs of trauma on the body?

"There was a large X cut into the victim's chest, but the coroner concluded that the incisions were made after the victim was dead. The cuts were very shallow; only a quarter of an inch deep with minimal bleeding."

"What do you make of the note left on the body?"

"I believe the killer is a religious wacko, taking an Old Testament passage literally. He probably believes he is an instrument of God. Religion and an unstable mind can be a lethal combination. This is no different than religious nuts blowing up abortion clinics."

"Very insightful, Detective Langford. Do you have any suspects in the case?

"I interviewed a retired homicide detective named Hank Moran who has a plausible theory on the murders. He said a traveling preacher named Reverend Brantley gave tent revivals in or near the same cities as the murders so he was around on the nights they were committed. The reverend has the same bible verse on his travel trailer. And one of his favorite rants is about the abomination of homosexuality. He has a stepbrother with a mental disorder who sometimes shows up at the revivals. Both the reverend and his stepbrother resemble the police sketch from Biloxi. When we completed our sketch it also resembled the person in the Biloxi sketch. Mr. Moran said there are way too many coincidences involving the preacher."

"I am acquainted with Detective Moran and his feelings about ignoring coincidences. Well, that is all I need for now, detective. You have been very helpful. Here is my card. I expect you to keep my office informed of any further developments in your investigation. If the copy of your file is ready I will leave you to your work."

Chapter 19

Sunday, July 18th, 2010

Sunday morning was quiet and peaceful for the Morans. Helen solved the crossword puzzle in the Sunday paper and Hank busied himself with some light maintenance on the motor home. He checked tire pressures, emptied the holding tanks, and refilled the fresh water holding tank to just above half full. He figured a half-full tank was enough water for traveling rather than carrying the weight of a full tank. The less weight carried by the motor home the better the gas mileage.

The rest of the morning was uneventful except for the call from Bill Anspach informing him the FBI was getting into the act. No murders were reported on the noon news show. All quiet in the Tri-Cities.

The Morans spent most of the afternoon in the Bristol Mall. Helen wanted to shop for a new set of Teflon-coated pans as the old ones from their kitchen in Kenner were quite worn. A bluegrass band was playing on the center stage in the mall and they stopped and listened for an hour. The banjo and fiddle players were excellent musicians. Bluegrass was Hank's favorite music genre.

On the way back to the motor home they swung into the Cedar Springs Campground near Fall Branch. The preacher's trailer was parked in site number twenty-two. His truck, however, was gone.

They arrived back at their campground around four. Helen prepared a light dinner with the new cookware. They turned on the five o'clock news while they ate. No reports of murders.

After dinner Hank and Helen took a stroll around the campground. They marveled at how friendly the fellow campers were and stopped to chat numerous times. One couple told them how much they enjoyed being full-timers. They sold their house, put a few things in storage, bought a new Tiffin, and were on the road two years now. Helen said she wasn't ready to give up their home base yet as they had only had their motor home for a few weeks and were just starting to feel comfortable in it.

When they returned to their Bounder there was a note taped to their motor home's door. Hank removed it wearing a pair of latex gloves that he used to handle the rig's sewer hose. The note read:

Mr. Moran,
Why don't you enjoy life and stop playing detective? I am sure you want to live long enough to have a long and happy retirement.
A friend

They went into the motor home and put the note and the duct tape it was fastened with into a plastic bag.

Monday July 19th, 2010

Dade City, Florida

Jason Cook, half-owner of Cook Brothers Construction Company stopped to unlock the front gate of the business. Exiting his truck and approaching the gate he noticed the padlock was just hanging in the hasp and unlocked. He swore under his breath and vowed to ream out the employee that was the last to leave on Friday, and then he realized it had been him. The large German Shepherd watchdog named Ripper appeared and followed Jason's truck. On passing the explosives storage shed he noticed the padlock was missing. He stopped the truck and checked out the shed. Upon entering the shed he noticed the top removed from a box of dynamite. Eight sticks were missing. Checking further he found six blasting caps and three wireless detonators also gone. Jason always kept a close watch on the inventory and knew exactly what should be in stock.

He chained up Ripper and headed to the office to report the break-in. His employees would not exit their autos if

Ripper was running loose. Ripper could sense their fear and seemingly enjoyed adding to it. The Dade City Police had a car on the scene in twenty minutes. The officer stated the theft had to be reported to the ATF field office in Tampa. They would have an agent on scene within the hour. The Dade City officer asked the usual routine questions and then proceeded to wait for the ATF agent.

An ATF agent by the name of Haas arrived and asked to see the storage shed. Jason assured him that all the explosives he had were legal and that he was a licensed user. He felt he was being investigated rather than the burglary. When Agent Haas was satisfied with the preliminaries he asked if Jason suspected any of his employees. Jason said he had seven employees and absolutely trusted all of them. Besides none of them would have risked entering the gate if Ripper was turned loose.

Agent Haas asked, "Is Ripper the large dog chained by the garage?"

Jason answered, "That's him. My people won't even get out of their cars in the morning unless he's chained."

"What about past employees?"

"No, I don't think . . . hey, wait a minute. I had a fella working for me awhile back that had an uncanny knack with the dog. He was the only one besides me who could get near Ripper. He could walk up to him and pet him and everything."

"What was his name and how long ago was this?"

"His name was Calvin Bixler. I had to let him go a little over a year ago. He just couldn't get along with anyone, except the dog that is."

"Anybody else come to mind?"

"No, not that I can think of. He was the only one I hired in the last two years. Everyone else has been here longer."

Agent Haas obtained the address and phone number the construction firm had on record for Calvin and was on his way to Zephyrhills. He stopped at the Wood Dale Mobile Home Park office to inquire about Calvin. The manager told him that the Bixlers had not lived there since the old man hanged himself about a year before. He didn't know where Calvin moved to. He did remember that Calvin had a stepbrother by the name of White-something who worked on the Jacksonville Bomb Squad.

Agent Haas thanked the manager and drove back to his office in Tampa. He went online and found the number for the Jacksonville Sheriff's Office. He asked the dispatcher if they had a bomb squad officer by the name of White. She said no, but they had a Sergeant Franklin Whitehead who led the squad. Haas was put through to Franklin.

"Sergeant Whitehead? This is ATF Agent Haas from down in Tampa. Do you have a stepbrother named Calvin Bixler?"

"Yes, I do, Agent Haas. Why is ATF interested in Calvin?"

"We just need to locate him and verify his whereabouts over the weekend."

"C'mon, Agent Haas, it sounds like your checking on an alibi for something."

"Sergeant, there was a theft of some explosives at a construction firm your stepbrother used to work for. We are routinely checking on all past employees of the firm. Do you have an address for him?"

"He lives in a travel trailer, and he has it parked at the Live Oaks RV Park on the south side of Ocala. I have his cell number if you want it."

"Yes, I would like his number, sergeant. Has your stepbrother ever been in any trouble with the law?"

"Agent Haas, I only learned of Calvin's existence a year ago. I have no idea what his history might contain."

Franklin gave the agent Calvin's number and the call ended.

Franklin immediately tried to call Calvin but got no answer. He then dialed his brother, Billy. Billy recognized Franklin's number and answered, "Hello, brother. How are things in the world of bombs?"

"Funny you should ask that, Billy. It looks like our stepbrother was successful. Do you know where he is?"

"Last I saw him was down in Cleveland, Tennessee at one of my revivals. He said he would be back up here by late Monday."

"If you happen to talk with him, tell him an ATF agent wants to have a chat with him."

"How did they get his name already?"

"They are just routinely checking on all past employees for an alibi for last weekend."

"I see. You still planning to help out up here?"

"Seems the least I can do is lend a hand for such a worthy cause."

"Thank you, brother. How are things going in Jacksonville? You and that real estate gal getting hitched yet?"

"Not yet, but we seem to be hitting it off pretty well. She does have some concerns about my safety on the job and if she could handle the stress of not knowing if I would return home every evening."

"That was the same issue that prompted your divorce. Hope you can work it out. I'll tell Calvin you called when I hear from him. Gotta run; I have a meeting at one of the local churches up here."

"OK, Billy, take care."

ATF Agent Haas dialed the number of the Live Oaks Campground.

A sweet sounding girl answered.

"Live Oaks, can I help you?

"Yes, you can. I want to get in touch with a man named Calvin Bixler. I understand he is staying at your park."

"Yes, Calvin is a work camper here at Live Oaks. But I think he took a few weeks off for a trip to Tennessee."

"I see. Are you sure he is not there?"

"I am sure. I can see his site from the office window and it's empty."

"OK, miss. Thank you for the information."

He tried Calvin's cell phone number again with no luck.

Monday Evening, July 19th

Tri-Cities, Tennessee

Hank and Helen were sitting at the dinette discussing the note when Hank's cell phone rang. The number didn't look familiar to Hank, but he answered anyway.

"Hello, you've reached the Morans."

"Hello, is this Mr. Hank Moran?"

"Yes it is. Who is calling please?"

"Mr. Moran, this is Agent Emory from the FBI office in Knoxville. Do you have a few minutes to talk?"

"I am sure I can spare a few. Is this agent Chris Emory formerly of the New Orleans field office?"

"Yes it is, Mr. Moran. I heard you recently retired and then took your detective work on the road."

"Agent Emory, I assure you, my recent detective work was unplanned. By the way, how have you been doing since New Orleans?"

"Things actually turned out pretty well for me up here. I'm now the lead agent in the Knoxville field office. I actually owe you an apology, Mr. Moran. I said some nasty things about you five years ago that I shouldn't have and blamed my transfer on you. It was very unprofessional of me. And please, do call me Chris."

"No need to apologize, Chris. I've been called many things during my career in law enforcement and undoubtedly you will, too. And actually your transfer was for your own safety."

"What do you mean, Mr. Moran?"

"Please, call me Hank. At the time the brotherhood had you on their list for what you did to their fellow officers."

"I was never told about that, Hank. There's just one thing I want to know about what happened five years ago. What gave you the first clue officers Parker and Fleming were innocent?"

"Sneakers."

"What do you mean 'sneakers?'"

"According to the eye witnesses in the bank the robbers were wearing sneakers and their uniforms didn't fit. Officers in New Orleans take pride in their appearance.

They should have been wearing black oxfords and neat-fitting uniforms."

"They could have been real officers dressed down to look like common felons."

"They could have, Chris, but I thought my scenario was more viable. Have you ever met an intelligent bank robber? Anyone with any brains knows bank robbers are always caught."

"Guess you're right, Hank. I hate to change the subject but I need to talk with you about the recent spate of slayings of homosexual men. I was planning on stopping up there tomorrow morning. How about nine?"

"Sounds good, Chris. We're staying at the largest campground in Baileyton up on the north side."

When they ended the call Helen asked if that was his old buddy from the FBI.

Hank said, "Yeah, it was. Actually, I'm glad the Bureau is getting involved. It's awfully hard to conduct an investigation when you have no authority or resources to do it right."

Helen said, "I am glad the FBI is getting involved. I am really worried about the threatening note we found on our motor home."

"One thing we could do is ask the neighboring campers if they saw anyone put it there," Hank replied.

Most of the nearby campers were sitting out when Hank canvassed the area. The rigs where no one was sitting out were missing either the tow vehicles or the toads, and Hank figured no one was home at those sites. One of the neighbors remembered seeing a tall dark-haired man walk by. They said he didn't say anything, just nodded. They couldn't say if he approached the Morans' motor home as they were facing the opposite direction.

Hank thought with trepidation, *Tall dark haired man.*

Monday Night, July 19th

Cleveland, Tennessee

Calvin arrived back at the Cleveland KOA just after ten P.M. He parked next to his trailer. He brought in the green duffel bag from the truck and called Billy. Billy recognized Calvin's number and answered on the third ring.

"Hello, Calvin. Everything go as planned?"

"Went real smooth, Billy. I can't believe they had the same old lock on the gate. Their guard dog was even glad to see his old buddy after more than a year. I've got everything we need."

"Calvin, I got a call from Franklin and he said an ATF agent was trying to contact you. He said it was just a routine call checking on past employees about the robbery."

"Don't worry, Billy. I am sure it's just routine like Franklin said. There is no way to connect me to it."

"Hope you're right, Calvin. Hope you're right."

"Gotta go, Billy. I need some sleep. Been on the road all day and night. Oh, did you make my reservations at the target?"

"Sure did. It's all set."

"Good, I'll be up there by early tomorrow afternoon. Goodnight, brother."

Chapter 20

Tuesday, July 20th, 2010

FBI Agent Emory arrived at the Morans' RV site ten minutes early for the nine o'clock meeting. Hank was sitting at the site's picnic table enjoying his second cup of morning coffee. He rose and shook hands with the agent.

"Chris, welcome to our humble abode."

Emory quickly took in the new motor home, "Nice rig, Hank. I wouldn't exactly call it humble."

"Well, it does have all the comforts of home. It even comes with a great office," Hank said as he motioned toward the picnic table. "Please, have a seat, Chris. I'll have Helen pour some more coffee. You still take it black?"

Emory smiled, recalling Hank's uncanny knack for remembering the slightest details. "Yeah, I still take it black, Hank."

Helen brought out a tray with a thermos pot of coffee plus an extra cup and joined them at the table. After agent Emory introduced himself to Helen he was ready to get down to business.

Emory started by saying, "I am up to date on all three slayings. I talked with the three police departments involved and I had a meeting with Detective Langford in Chattanooga yesterday. All three victims were definitely gay. However the M.O. for the first murder in Gulf Breeze is not the same as the other two. The first victim was shot in the back of the head with a .38 and the other two were suffocated."

Hank said, "It could be the same killer just perfecting his art. Have you had time to analyze the three notes left on the victims?"

"The first note is slightly different than the other two. The numbers two and three in 20:13 appear to be written by a different person. In the first note the 2 is written with a loop and in the other two it isn't."

Helen asked, "Agent Emory, do you have copies of the three notes with you?"

"Yes I do, Mrs. Moran." Emory produced the three notes from his brief case.

Helen said to wait one minute and retrieved the plastic bag containing the threatening note from the motor home. "This is a note that was taped to our door last night. We think it was put there by the killer, or should I say, one of the killers."

Helen laid the note beside the other three notes and carefully scrutinized all four. She said, "I think the person who left the note on the first victim is the same person who taped the threat to our door. The 'L' and the 'E' look the same as the first note. And the 'F' and especially the word 'AND' do not match the third note."

"You have a good eye, Mrs. Moran. I'm inclined to agree with you."

"We do have three possible suspects so maybe there were two different killers," Hank said.

"Hank, the main reason I stopped in today was to find out all you know about the preacher and your reasons for your suspicion that he is involved."

Hank related the long tale to Agent Emory, from their short trip to Biloxi to the recent confrontation with Brantley. He then told Emory about the research Bill Anspach had done on the preacher and his brothers.

Emory asked for the cell phone numbers for Brantley and his brothers.

Hank stated he only had the number for Brantley. He told Emory he should be able to reach Franklin Whitehead at the Jacksonville Sheriff's Office. Emory confirmed the availability of WI-FI at the campground and pulled his laptop from his case. In two minutes he had the sheriff's office number.

Emory walked away from the picnic table and leaned against a tall oak tree. The Jacksonville Sheriff's Office answered after the second ring. Emory asked to speak with Franklin Whitehead. There was a short pause, and after a few more rings there was an answer.

"Sergeant Whitehead speaking."

"Sergeant, this is Agent Emory from the FBI's Knoxville field office. How are things on the bomb squad?"

"Thankfully it's been all quiet for the summer so far."

"Sergeant, the reason I am calling is I need some information on your stepbrother, Calvin Bixler. Do you happen to know how I could reach him?"

"Well, he's staying at an RV resort near Ocala. I talked with my brother, William, yesterday and he said he traveled up to see William last week and stayed at a KOA campground near Cleveland, Tennessee."

"Sergeant, do you have Calvin Bixler's cell phone number?"

Franklin gave the number to Emory. "Agent Emory, I gave the same information to ATF Agent Haas yesterday. Is your inquiry about the dynamite theft over the weekend?"

Hank watched Emory suddenly straighten up and take on a look of excitement.

Emory said, "No, this is a different matter. Tell me about the dynamite theft."

"Some dynamite was stolen from a construction firm down in Dade City. The ATF was routinely checking past employees. Apparently Calvin worked there about a year and a half ago."

"Have you talked with your stepbrother recently?"

"No, I tried to call him yesterday after the ATF agent's call but couldn't get through."

They chatted small talk for awhile then Emory thanked Franklin for the information and ended the call.

Emory thought Franklin was probably kicking himself in the ass for mentioning the dynamite theft.

As Emory approached the picnic table Hank spoke, "Chris, I couldn't help but overhear part of your conversation. Did I hear you mention a dynamite theft?"

"There was a robbery at a construction firm down in Dade City over the weekend. Calvin Bixler was a past employee of the firm and an ATF agent was making a routine check on him."

Helen said, "Fire and brimstone next. It looks like we should find Mr. Bixler."

"You used the word '*we*,' Mrs. Moran. I am afraid I have to ask you and Hank to stand down and leave the investigation to the Bureau. Especially since you were on the receiving end of that threatening note."

"We may take your advice on that. I don't want to put Helen in any more danger. What's your next step, Chris?"

"I plan to track down Mr. Bixler to see if he has any dynamite on board."

"Chris, may I suggest you obtain the cell phone call records of Calvin Bixler and Reverend Brantley? The records might provide a clue as to the target for the dynamite."

"That might be a little premature, Hank. You're already assuming Bixler stole the dynamite. You said you saw his trailer at the KOA last Friday morning."

"Chris, you know how I hate coincidences. I said I saw only his trailer. His truck was gone. There's no telling what time he left. He could have easily made it down to Dade City for the weekend robbery."

"OK, Hank, I'll look into it. I should know better than to doubt your intuition."

"It's not intuition, Chris. It's putting the facts together into a viable theory."

"OK, OK, Hank. I'll look into it. Meantime you and Mrs. Moran enjoy the rest of your trip."

"Will do, Chris. It's been good talking with you again, and good luck."

Emory handed his card to Hank and told him if he remembered anything else that would help to give him a call. They shook hands, and Emory left.

Helen said they needed to go in town to do a little grocery shopping. Hank said they had nothing better to do now that the cavalry had arrived. They hopped into the Honda and headed into town. Helen entered the small grocery store while Hank began filling the Honda's tank at the store's gas pump. Hank noticed some RVs heading up Route 172 towards the hills. Hank surmised the man on the other side of the pumps was a local. His bib overalls, wad of tobacco in his cheek, and old pickup truck with a confederate flag decal on the back window were the giveaways.

Hank asked the man, "Excuse me sir, is there an RV park up that way?"

The man answered, "The Timberfalls Resort is a few miles up the road."

"Hmm...My wife and I will have to drive up and check it out for future reference."

"I don't think it's a good idea to take your wife up there."

Just then Helen walked up with a small bag of groceries and heard the man's remark. "Not a good idea to take his wife where?" Helen asked.

"We was talkin' about the campground up the road ma'am. You see it's a place that only allows them queer fellers in."

"You mean there is actually a campground just for gay men?" Hank asked.

"It's not only a campground. I heard tell they have a big lodge and cabins and a big swimmin' pool, too. They tell me they're booked up tight for the whole summer. Must be *some* goins on."

That got the Moran's attention fast. Helen looked at Hank and asked, "You thinking what I'm thinking?"

"If you're thinking what I'm thinking then we're both thinking the same thing."

The man in the bibbies gave them a confused look, shook his head, mumbled something about danged tourists, and then replaced the gas nozzle back in the pump.

Hank paid for his gas and the Morans headed up Route 172 to find Timberfalls. A mile and a half up the road they found the entrance on the right. A small sign read: WELCOME TO TIMBERFALLS RESORT.

A four-hundred foot long gravel lane led up to the guardhouse and the simple iron pipe gate. Hank pulled to the side next to the guardhouse window. A big burly attendant slid the window open.

The attendant asked, "You folks lose your way?"

Hank said, "No, not really. We were just out driving around and heard there was a campground up here. We just wanted to check it out for future reference."

"Well, folks, I don't think you would be interested in our facility. This is a men only resort and the lady wouldn't be welcome."

Helen asked, "You mean it's a men's hunting lodge of some sort?"

The attendant grinned widely and said, "Well ma'am, I guess you could call it a hunting lodge of sorts. But not the type you're referring to. You see this resort only caters to men of a certain persuasion."

Hank said, "Hmm, I have a friend who might be interested in your resort. Do you have a brochure we could send to him?"

The attendant handed them a brochure and an insert that had the resort's events calendar for the summer. Hank thanked him and the attendant said they could make a U-turn behind the guard house. While Hank was negotiating the turn Helen was looking out her side window and caught a glimpse of the RV park.

"Hank! There's a naked man down there in front of a motor home!

Hank laughed and said, "Helen, something tells me there's more than one in the area. I guess you couldn't see the attendant we were talking to was wearing a leather vest and chaps."

Helen just uttered, "Oh my."

Helen looked through the brochure on the drive back to Baileyton.

"Hank, they're having a Mr. Timberfalls contest this weekend. It's supposed to be the biggest bash of the year."

"Helen, do you think I should enter the contest and case the joint to see if Calvin shows up?"

Helen laughed and said, "Hank, dear, you wouldn't stand a chance. You're not hairy enough. And besides, you don't have a little Speedo to wear. You should see some of these pictures! They give a Web site at the bottom. We'll have to get online when we get back to the Bounder."

As the Morans parked next to their motor home Helen noticed a white envelope stuck to the Bounder's door.

"Look at the door, Hank, another note."

"Don't touch it, Helen! I'll get a pair of gloves."

Hank retrieved another pair of latex gloves from the Bounder's storage area and proceeded to unfasten the envelope. The front of the envelope just said *The Morans*.

Hank opened the envelope, unfolded the note that was inside and laughed. It was just a note from the park management informing them of the weekly rate at the campground if they decide to stay more than the three nights of their reservation.

Helen breathed a sigh of relief and suggested they better sign up for it as the big bash at Timberfalls wasn't until the weekend.

Tuesday Afternoon, July 20th, 2010

Calvin approached the guardhouse gate at the Timberfalls Resort and was greeted by the attendant.

"Welcome to Timberfalls. Do you have a reservation?"

Calvin was amused as to how a big hairy guy could have such a feminine voice.

"Yes, I have a reservation. The name's Bentley."

"OK, Mr. Bentley, I see you are on the list. Please pull ahead to the office and they will set you up with a site."

"Oh, before I forget. I will be having a guest arrive by the name of Whitner. I would appreciate if you let him through."

"That's too bad, Mr. Bentley."

"What's too bad?"

"It's too bad you're having a guest for your stay. We could always use a few more singles," the attendant said with a wink.

Calvin smiled, pulled through the gate, and stopped at the registration office.

"Good afternoon, sir. Your name, please?"

"My name's Bentley and I have a reservation."

"Oh, here we go, Mr. Bentley. We have you back in the Heights RV Park. Just follow the map. You are in site number fifteen. We have your reservation for five nights. Is that correct?"

"That's right."

"And how do you wish to pay? The total comes to two-hundred and thirty-two dollars."

After telling them about his expected guest, Calvin paid with cash, and proceeded to the Heights RV Park.

Calvin attracted a small audience while he backed his trailer into the RV site. He performed the maneuver with perfection on the first try. The audience applauded when Calvin exited his truck. He took a bow and smiled.

A man in his mid-twenties with sandy colored hair and wearing a flowery shirt and shorts approached, "You're the first one this afternoon to back in on the first try. Thanks to you I just won thirty bucks."

"Aha, a betting pool on arriving campers. I was wondering what the audience was all about."

"You're welcome to join the betting pool. It's all in good fun."

"Thanks for offering, but I'll take a rain check on that. My first priority is to check out the swimming pool and get a cool drink," Calvin replied.

"We were all going to head down to the pool ourselves. Here we all are being unsocial. My name's Dewayne and yours is . . .?"

"My name's Calvin. And who are your friends?"

The small group introduced themselves to Calvin. Calvin had a hard time remembering names and decided it was fruitless to try. Although he figured he wouldn't forget the big hairy Italian looking guy who said his name was Sally. He said it was short for Salvatore but Sally sounded like the fitting moniker when he talked.

They said Calvin should just grab his swim pants. He could change in the shower house. Sally suggested that with the pool being clothing optional, swim pants were unnecessary. Calvin retrieved his swim pants from the Denali fifth wheel and the small group headed down the path to the pool and tiki bar.

Agent Emory was mulling over all the information he accumulated on the three hate crimes. In a quandary as to what to do next he kept coming back to Hank's theory that the preacher and his kin were somehow involved. Hank was right: there were too many coincidences. He decided to call the ATF office in Tampa and talk with Agent Haas.

"Agent Haas? Agent Emory of the FBI."

"Yes, Agent Emory, what can I do for you?"

"I am working a case that might be related to the dynamite theft in Dade City over the weekend. Have you made any progress on the theft?"

"We have one person of interest by the name of Calvin Bixler, but we have not been able to locate him. All the present employees of the construction firm checked out. Bixler is a person of interest due to his ability to befriend the construction firm's watchdog. The only other person able to control the dog was the owner and we have no reason to suspect him. We checked on Bixler's cell phone number and found his account was canceled last Thursday up in Cleveland, Tennessee."

Emory offered, "The last time Bixler was seen was last Thursday in Cleveland. His camper trailer was seen in the KOA on Friday.

"Is the trailer still there?"

"I don't know, but I will check right away."

When Emory was through with Agent Haas he called the Cleveland KOA. They said they hadn't seen Bixler around for a few days but his rig was gone early that morning.

They said a fellow camper named Moran had also called and wanted the same information.

Emory asked when Mr. Moran called and they said about an hour before.

Emory called Agent Haas back and gave him the update on Bixler. The fact that he wasn't seen for a few days lent credence to the possibility that he could have traveled to Dade City during that time. Emory thought, *Damn, Moran might be right again. And what in hell is he doing? I asked him to stand down.*

Not knowing Bixler's present location Emory decided it was time to have a chat with his stepbrother, Reverend Billy Brantley. But first he wanted to talk with Hank Moran.

Hank recognized the number when his cell phone rang. "Hello, Chris."

"Hank, I thought I asked you to stand down on the investigation."

"You did, Chris, but something came up. I just tried to call you but your line was busy."

"What came up, Hank?"

Hank told Emory about their visit to the Timberfalls Resort and that it could be a possible target for the dynamite.

"Chris, did you have any luck in locating Bixler?"

"Not yet. We did find his phone company and his account was canceled."

"Yeah, we found that out when we tried to call him. It said the number was no longer in service."

"Hank, you lied to me. You said you didn't have his number."

"We didn't have it, Chris. Helen saw it written on your note pad on our picnic table this morning."

"I can't believe this. I not only have to put up with you, but now you have a partner, too."

"The best I ever had, Chris. Oh and, Chris, may I suggest you put out a highway alert to see if Mr. Bixler is still in this area or on his way home to Ocala? His rig should be very easy to spot. If he was heading home he'd be halfway through Georgia on Interstate 75."

"Is there anything else, Hank?"

"Not at the moment, Chris. Talk to you later."

When Hank disconnected he said to Helen, "Some people you just have to lead around by the nose."

Helen said, "Hank, do you realize that if Bixler left the KOA in Cleveland early this morning he might already be at Timberfalls?"

"I thought the same thing, Helen, but what can we do about it?"

"I might have a plan, Hank."

Chapter 21

Tuesday, July 20th, 2010

Agent Emory called Reverend Brantley's number late in the afternoon. Emory introduced himself as an FBI investigator when Brantley answered.

"Why in the world is the FBI calling me?" Brantley responded.

"Reverend, I need to sit down and talk with you about some murders that occurred over the last few weeks. They seem to coincide with your tent revival ministries."

Brantley replied, "I only heard of those murders recently from a gentleman named Moran and his wife. They as good as accused me of being a murderer. You're certainly welcome to come and sit down and talk if it would help you deal with those heinous crimes. We could even offer a prayer or two to ask for the Lord's help."

"Thank you, Reverend. You are most kind. I would like to meet with you within the hour if at all possible."

"I think that would fit into my schedule, Agent Emory. I am staying at the Cedar Springs Campground near Fall Branch. RV site number twenty-two."

"I think I can find that, Reverend. I am on my way."

"I'll be here waiting for you, Agent Emory."

Emory entered the campground's address into his GPS unit and arrived at Brantley's site twenty minutes later.

He had spent the last hour at the Mountain Missionary Church interviewing the minister and his wife. The Mountain Missionary Church was the site of Brantley's last revival meeting. They claimed the revival was successful and Reverend Brantley's presentation was very motivating. Attendance was up for the normal Sunday service. The only negative aspect was that he dwelt too long on the Old Testament, especially Leviticus. Their church and mission is geared more for the teachings of Christ and the New

Testament. Other than that they recalled no strange or abnormal happenings during the revival.

Emory parked his government issue blue Ford Crown Vic in the empty site next to Brantley's. Brantley was waiting for him in a lawn chair under the trailer's awning. He remained seated as Emory approached. Emory introduced himself, and Brantley offered him a seat in the other folding chair.

Brantley said, "I didn't mean to be inhospitable, but I had a back spasm earlier in the day and have to remain seated."

Emory said, "That's no problem, Reverend. I had one a few years ago and know just how you feel. Reverend, I need to ask you a few pointed questions. These are of a routine nature when investigating a crime such as murder. Right now you are on our list as a person of interest in the investigation. The sooner we get the questioning over with the sooner you come off the list."

"I understand, Agent Emory. You may ask away."

"Reverend Brantley, were you aware that there was a gay man by the name of Jesse Lutz murdered in Gulf Breeze, Florida the day after your Pensacola revival?"

"No, I was not aware of that at the time."

"Reverend, were you aware that there was a gay man by the name of Donald Fleet murdered the night of your revival in Biloxi, Mississippi?"

Brantley replied, "No, I was not aware of that at the time."

"Reverend, were you aware that there was a murder of a gay man named Anthony Edwards the same night as your revival in Cleveland, Tennessee?"

"No, I was not aware of that at the time. I only found out about the murders from Mr. Moran a few days ago."

"Reverend, I see you have the Leviticus 20:13 bible verse on the side of your trailer. Are you aware that the killer planted a note on each victim with the same verse printed on it?"

"I was not aware of that until Mr. Moran mentioned it a few days ago."

"Reverend, how do you explain the connection of your ministry to all the things I just mentioned?"

"Agent Emory, I have no explanation for it other than that there must be a very sick person involved to do those horrid things. I've been praying every night since I heard of the murders for God to intervene and stop them. Perhaps he heard my prayers; there hasn't been another murder up in this area."

"I hope you're right. Reverend, I have three pictures I would like you to look at and comment on."

Emory removed the three composite sketches of the murder suspects from his folder and laid them out on the small table. Reverend Brantley looked at the drawings and showed no emotion.

"The only thing I can say, Agent Emory, is the faces on the sketches do have a very slight resemblance to my brothers and me. You know as well as I that there could be thousands of others who have the same slight resemblance."

"Since you mentioned your brothers, Reverend, do you know where your stepbrother, Calvin, is?"

"The last I saw Calvin was down in Cleveland. He said he had to get back to his job in Florida."

"So you have no idea of his whereabouts at the moment?"

"Agent Emory, I am not my brother's keeper. He does as he pleases."

"Reverend, an ATF agent from Tampa would like to contact him about a dynamite theft at his former place of employment. Do you have a way of contacting him?"

"I am aware of the agent's wishes. My brother, Franklin, called and informed me. As of now I have no way of contacting my stepbrother. It seems his number is no longer in service."

"Don't all of these coincidences seem questionable to you, Reverend?"

"I am sure they are just coincidences, Agent Emory. I am a man of God, not an experienced criminal investigator. I am sure you will figure it all out in due time."

"That I will, Reverend. That I will. Thank you for your cooperation. We may need to have another chat later."

"I will be here for only a few more days, Agent Emory. You can always reach me on my cell."

Emory called it a day and made the long drive back to his home in Knoxville. He had a hard time reading the reverend. He had seemingly polished responses, but those could have been due to his oratory ability from years of preaching. Yet he had a feeling that the reverend wasn't being entirely truthful.

Timberfalls, Tuesday, July 20th

Calvin was so relaxed from his swim that he fell asleep in a chaise on the deck of the tiki bar. Dewayne let him sleep for over an hour then nudged his shoulder. Calvin awoke and was presented with a frosted margarita.

"I thought you would like something cool to drink," Dewayne said.

"Thank you, Dewayne," Calvin said. "You sure know how to treat a guy."

Dewayne immediately brightened up when he got a positive response from Calvin. He had been attracted to Calvin the minute he pulled into the campground with his rig. It took Dewayne a few minutes to work up the courage to ask the question.

"Hey, Cal, are you with someone? I guess I mean do you have a partner?"

The question floored Calvin as he had never been in this situation before. He thought a minute before he could come up with an answer that would not give him away.

"No, Dewayne, I don't have a partner and I'm not living with anyone if that's what you mean. I lived with my father until he recently passed away. Since then I've been living by myself in my trailer."

Dewayne said, "I did have a very close friend I was living with down in Biloxi, but we had a misunderstanding and I got mad and walked out. The next night he went out drinking and met up with the wrong guy and got himself murdered."

An alarm immediately went off in Calvin's head. "When did that happen, Dewayne?"

"It was ten days ago. His name was Donny Fleet. I kept blaming myself because if I hadn't walked out on him he'd still be alive. He wouldn't have gone out drinking. My friends thought it would be a good idea for me to come up here to try to forget."

Calvin said, "You have to stop blaming yourself, Dewayne. Your friend was a grown man and was responsible for his own actions. He got himself into trouble because he just made a few bad decisions."

"You talk like you knew him, Calvin."

Calvin thought to himself, *If only you knew Dewayne, If only you knew.*

"I didn't know him, Dewayne, but I knew a few like him. My father was one. He made many very bad decisions that eventually cost him his life."

Calvin said he was tired. That he had a very long day and was heading back to his trailer. He told Dewayne he would touch base with him tomorrow. On the walk back to his trailer Calvin was deeply disturbed trying to reason why he had encountered Dewayne. Was it just coincidence or was it a synergy perpetrated by God. He needed to call his stepbrother Billy for guidance but Billy had told him to call only in an extreme emergency.

He went to bed pondering the recent events. He also puzzled over his feelings for Dewayne. Confusing feelings he did not understand. He had a very restless night's sleep.

Timberfalls, Wednesday, July 21st

Hank drove the Bounder up to the gate house at Timberfalls. Fortunately there was a different gate attendant than yesterday. This attendant was fully clothed and had a name pin on his shirt that said "Mikey." Hank gave his name as Mr. Morgan and stated he had a reservation that was just made yesterday. The attendant found his name on the list and passed him on through the gate.

Hank's next stop was at the registration office. The office clerk said he was fortunate to get a site on such short notice. They had someone cancel and had an opening up in the new Heavens RV Park. Hank paid cash for a four night stay. He asked the clerk if anybody named Bixler had registered the day before. The clerk took a moment to look over the registration ledger then shook his head. He didn't see a registration for anyone by that name.

The clerk handed Hank a new arrival package which included a Timberfalls property map and a pamphlet on all the upcoming activities. He said to Hank, "Mr. Morgan, I think it's great that the elderly are still interested in the activities we have to offer here at Timberfalls,"

Hank smiled and said, "I'm still a youngster at heart."

"I bet you are, Mr. Morgan. Just follow the map to the upper campground and you are in site number seventeen."

Hank followed the winding road through the main parking lot, past the barn and corral, past the tavern, then into the Heights RV Park. He followed the map through the Heights and saw the road leading to the Heavens RV Park at the far end. The Heavens was a new section that had just opened the year before. Hank thought it was odd that he had to drive through one park to get to the other but he figured it saved them from building an additional road through the forested property.

Hank maneuvered the motor home into the upper park and found site seventeen. It was a nice wide gravel back-in site with some newly grown grass in the picnic table area. Someone had parked a small KIA in the empty site which blocked entry. Hank blew the horn and a guy rushed out of the class C Winnebago in the adjacent site. He was all apologetic and ran to move the KIA. Hank noticed the awning next door was strung with a set of pink flamingo party lights. His only thought was, *What in hell are we getting into?*

Once his site was cleared Hank backed in and shut off the engine. Helen appeared from hiding in the rear bathroom. Her plan was to remain in the Bounder until dark. Then dressed as legitimately as possible as a small man she would be free to explore the resort with Hank. "So far so good," she said to Hank. Hank said he couldn't wait to see her in her evening attire. Helen said she hoped he wouldn't get too turned on. Hank said he'll try to hold himself back. Helen said he should go out and connect up the lines. She hoped he wouldn't get propositioned in the process.

They had opted for the weekly rate at the Baileyton campground so they left the Honda parked there rather than towing it up to Timberfalls. All Hank had to do was connect the power and water lines, the sewer hose, and the TV cable, and he was all set. Once back inside all they had to do was extend the slides.

Hank was connecting the water line when the neighbor with the pink flamingo awning lights came over and apologized again for parking in his site. Hank assured him that it was no problem.

"Are you here by yourself?" the man asked.

"Momentarily", Hank replied. "I am having a guest arrive later this evening."

"Gee, that's too bad. We're having a little party later on down in the other campground and we have a few other singles. After the party we'll head to the tavern and dance floor. Of course, you and your guest are invited."

Hank said, "Thanks for the invitation. But we'll have to wait and see how tired my guest is when he arrives."

Hank finished his connections as fast as possible and retreated back into the Bounder.

Earlier that morning

Calvin awoke late and realized he had a lot of exploring to do before his stepbrother arrived. He had to find the ideal spot for the dynamite charge. A placement where it would do the most damage. Franklin said he would arrive late in the afternoon. He agreed to set the charge that night for Calvin on the condition that he could be gone in the morning. The actual detonation would then be at Calvin's choosing.

Calvin stopped briefly outside his fifth wheel trailer to study the resort's property map. When he started walking down the path to the main lodge he found Dewayne was by his side.

"Hey, Cal, whatcha doin?"

"Morning, Dewayne. I thought I'd do some exploring today and see what this place is all about."

"Mind if I join ya, Cal? I haven't seen everything yet myself."

"Sure, Dewayne. I'll be glad for the company."

Their first stop was the main lodge. It was a large rustic building of log construction with a large front deck. The deck afforded a view of a two acre pond and beyond the pond was the tiki bar and swimming pool. A pair of Canadian geese were swimming in the pond with a string of five small goslings following the mother.

Dewayne followed Calvin into the lodge. The first thing Calvin noticed was the high vaulted ceiling in the lobby and an enormous stone fireplace. There was ample seating for a number of guests to enjoy the fire on a cold winter's day. However, being a hot July morning the hearth was filled with potted ferns and most of the guests were either at the pool or hiking along the cool forested trails.

Calvin caught the odor of food cooking and asked Dewayne if he'd had breakfast. Dewayne said he hadn't so Calvin said it was his treat. They were shown to a table in the dining area. Dewayne opted for waffles covered with strawberries and whipped cream while Calvin settled for basic scrambled eggs, sausage, and toast.

While Calvin ate he watched a few lodge guests come and go. Some hand in hand. An ornamental wooden staircase led to the upper floors which contained the dozen or so guest rooms.

He concluded that the main lodge was not a heavily concentrated gathering place. After breakfast Calvin paid the bill and left a generous tip.

"Where to next?" Dewayne asked.

Calvin said, "I've already seen the pool and tiki bar. Let's check out the barn and that other rooming house called the Annex."

The barn looked just like its namesake. It was converted to a dormitory to house the peak season staff that lived on campus. The Annex was a nondescript building with seven guest rooms and a shower room for the nearby tent camping area.

On the way back up the hill towards the RV park Calvin caught site of the tavern. "Have you been in the tavern yet, Dewayne?"

"Yeah, I was in it two nights ago. It's a nice big place with a big dance floor and all, but I felt uncomfortable there and didn't stay long."

"Why did you feel uncomfortable there, Dewayne?"

"I guess it was because it was the type of bar that my friend, Donny, was drinking in the night he was murdered. It just brought back bad feelings."

"I see, well I'm going to go inside and look it over and maybe have an early beer. You coming along?"

"I guess I will, Cal. I need to get over things."

Dewayne followed Calvin into the tavern. It was a large establishment. About the size of some nightclubs Calvin had seen in the big cities. It had all the accoutrements of a standard night club. It sported a thirty foot long bar lined with stools, a large table area with seating for a hundred, and a comparable sized dance floor. The stage at the far end of the dance floor was large enough for a six-piece band with a DJ set-up on the left side.

Calvin and Dewayne slid onto bar stools and Calvin ordered two drafts. There were three other patrons at a table getting an early start on the day's drinking. Calvin asked the bartender with the name tag "Jake" if the tavern was crowded at night. Jake said he had a full house nearly every night since the middle of June.

One of the guys at the table said they should have been here last night. "A few of the contestants for the Mr. Timberfalls contest arrived and put on a little prelim show."

Calvin said he was sorry he missed it. He turned to the bartender and said he had an offer for a partnership at a new nightclub down if Florida. He said with such a large dance floor there must be heavy beams to support the load. The bartender said the dance floor was supported by heavy timbers in the basement. He added that the basement opened onto the lower driveway and that all the deliveries were made into the lower level. Calvin asked how the kegs of beer were brought upstairs. The bartender replied that he had a small elevator at the end of the bar big enough for a man and a keg on a hand truck.

Calvin said that was very interesting thanked Jake the bartender and left him a two dollar tip.

Chapter 22

Wednesday, July 21st, 2010 – Timberfalls Resort

It was late afternoon at Timberfalls when Hank told
Helen he was going for a walk to see if Calvin had showed
up in one of the campgrounds. Sporting a blue Grateful
Dead dancing skeletons T-shirt, khaki cargo shorts, brown
sandals, and panama hat, he thought he might fit in as he
started his walk. Looking around he discovered he might
be overdressed as he spotted a few guys dressed only in
sandals and their birthday suits. He was glad Helen didn't
have a panoramic view of the campground from their site.

He did receive a few comments on his outfit such as,
"Hey pops, like your shirt." Hank just smiled and said
thanks. He stood in the middle of the Heavens Park and
turning 360 degrees he could see all of the rigs. Calvin's
was not among them.

As he entered the lower Heights Park he looked to his
right down the row of campers and spotted a black F-250.
He had to get a closer look so he walked down the row of
RV sites. He received more comments about his shirt as he
passed campers lounging outside their rigs, most with long
neck beer bottles in hand. One even asked if he had
anything interesting in all the pockets in his cargo shorts.
Hank replied, "Just car keys, no frogs or snakes." The
inquisitor said he'd like to find a big long snake. There was
laughter from the small group.

Hank approached the rig with the black pick-up parked
in front and saw that it was a Denali fifth wheel. He
remembered Calvin's tag number from down in Cleveland
so he walked around to the back of the F-250. The tag was
a match.

Hank looked up and saw a tall, thin, dark haired
familiar figure approaching. It looked like Reverend
Brantley walking up the road from the parking lot. Visitors
had to park in the main lot as there was limited parking for

146

only one vehicle at the RV sites. Hank quickly walked to the edge of the park where he would be partially hidden by a clump of azalea bushes whose springtime blooms had long ago vanished. As the man got closer Hank kept thinking it was the preacher but something was different. He thought back to that Saturday in Biloxi where he saw changes in the appearance of the preacher from morning to afternoon. Hank then realized he may indeed have been seeing two different people. He retrieved his cell phone from a pocket in his cargo shorts and called the preacher's number that he had saved in his directory. As the phone was ringing on the other end he thought, "Now let's see who answers the call."

"Reverend Brantley speaking." The phone was not answered by the person now knocking on Calvin's trailer door. Hank managed a short "Sorry, wrong number," then disconnected. He realized the visitor must be the preacher's twin brother, Franklin Whitehead. Hank's uncanny knack for remembering seemingly insignificant details had paid off once again. The addition of Franklin, who was an explosives expert, into the picture brought it into sharper focus.

Hank immediately clicked on Agent Emory's number in his cell phone's directory. Emory's automated answering service asked the caller to please leave a message.

"Chris, this is Hank Moran. I am camped in the Timberfalls resort near Baileyton. Calvin Bixler is camped here and his stepbrother, Franklin Whitehead, just showed up. I am sure this is their next target. You better get up here!"

Calvin answered the door and invited his stepbrother in. They greeted each other with a brief handshake. Calvin asked, "Do you want a beer Frankie?"

Franklin replied, "I need one real bad. I've been on the road since six in the morning and ran into heavy traffic around Atlanta. Well Calvin, what have you come up with?"

"I checked out all the buildings, Frankie, and the one that looks the most promising is the tavern. It has a large dance floor and access to the basement underneath. The bartender said he has had a full house most every night since mid-June."

"Do you think we could get into the basement tonight?"

"I'm sure we can. There is an elevator at the end of the bar that's used to bring up kegs and cases of beer from the basement. I am sure I can convince the bartender to let us take a ride on it. I told him we are planning to open a club in Florida and would like to install an elevator just like his."

"OK, Cal, I'm gonna get a few hours of shuteye then we will go and check out this tavern. By the way, where are the goodies?"

"They are up underneath the bed in a duffel bag."

"Uh, I think I'll take my nap down here on the sofa-bed."

Hank's cell phone rang as he was walking back to his motor home. It was Agent Emory returning his call. "Hank, this is Chris. I got your message. It sounds like you are still on the hunt."

"You're right, Chris. An old dog like me doesn't give up when he's on the scent."

"You said in your message that you located Bixler and his stepbrother, Whitehead?"

"You heard right; they're both up here presently holed up in Bixler's trailer. We need someone to eyeball them."

"I'll tell you what, Hank. I have a man on stakeout over at the preacher's campground. He could be there within the hour."

"I think that would be wise, Chris. I'm sure this is where the action is. The preacher is most likely the planner. He probably coerced Bixler into the dirty deeds. You know about Bixler's mental problem?"

"Yes, I do, Hank. Promise me you'll stand back and let us do our job. At the moment we have no probable cause to garner a search warrant. Just a pile of coincidences and theory. Only thing we can do is keep a close watch and see what materializes. Contrary to popular belief, even in homeland security we just can't raid the place without probable cause."

"I understand, Chris. I'll talk to you later."

Hank proceeded back to the Bounder and updated Helen on what he saw and the gist of his conversation with Agent Emory. Helen listened intently then offered, "Hank, we're not FBI or homeland security." Hank looked at Helen and said, "Don't even think it."

One hour later Hank was getting fidgety. He told Helen that he was talking with some of the other campers earlier and they said the place with the largest gathering of people was the tavern; big crowd most every night. Helen suggested he walk down and look it over. "But be back in an hour for dinner," she said.

Hank was walking past the Heights campground on his way to the tavern when he heard a voice say, "Hey mister, hold up a minute."

Hank stopped, turned and saw a man in his mid-twenties with a medium build and sandy colored hair approach. "What is it you want?" Hank asked.

"I saw you watching my friend's trailer earlier. I just thought I'd let you know that."

"Which friend do you mean?" asked Hank.

"My friend, Calvin Bentley, in the Denali fifth wheel."

"You're Calvin's friend? How long have you known him?"

"Oh, I just met him a couple of days ago and we have been having the start of a relationship. That is until his guest showed up."

"I am sure you don't have to worry about Calvin's guest. I don't think he will harm your relationship with Calvin. By the way my name is Hank, what's yours?"

"I'm Dewayne. What did you mean about Calvin's guest?"

"Well, Dewayne, his guest is his stepbrother from Florida. And if you are planning a relationship with Calvin I think you should know his real name."

"His real name? I don't understand."

"His last name in Bixler, not Bentley."

"How do you know so much about Calvin?"

"I can't tell you anymore right now, Dewayne. But I can tell you to be very careful around Calvin. Always have other people around when you are with him."

"Hank, what do you mean about being careful?"

"That's all I can tell you, Dewayne. I have to go."

Hank left Dewayne standing there looking mystified.

On his way to the tavern Hank was thinking that he planted a seed with Dewayne. If he did have a budding relationship with Calvin like he said they had, he was sure Dewayne would inquire about his last name. And Calvin would wonder how anyone in the campground would know. It might be enough to scare them off and avoid a disaster. All he had to do was catch them with the explosives before they had the chance to use them.

Hank entered the tavern and looked around. It was early evening and the place was still nearly empty. Just a half dozen guests sitting at the bar and a couple of tables. He liked the quaint atmosphere of the place and thought it would be nice a nice place to enjoy an evening if it was an establishment meant for heterosexuals.

Hank could see that the tavern would be the perfect target, especially with a packed house and dance floor. He enjoyed one beer then headed back to the motor home as Helen should have had dinner nearly ready.

Helen was preparing a microwave dinner for two when there was a knock on the door. She opted not to answer the door. She had not planned to don her disguise until after dinner and she dared not to answer the door and have the caller know there was a female in the resort.

The knocking stopped and Helen assumed the caller had left. Five minutes later she peeked out the kitchen curtain and noticed a man standing near the front of the Bounder behind a bush that separated the sites. He was wearing shorts and a loose shirt. When he bent over slightly to swat a bug that landed on his leg Helen noticed a gun that was tucked in the back of his belt under his shirt.

Helen glanced out the front window and noticed Hank approaching. As Hank drew closer she saw the man reach behind his back. She immediately thought of the threatening note that was recently left on their door. The only weapon Helen could come up with fast was a cast iron skillet sitting on top of the gas stove. Grabbing the skillet she bounded out the door with skillet raised. The startled man turned, quickly stepped back, and tripped over the water connection stanchion for the next site. He landed hard on his back and his eyesight went momentarily fuzzy. He was sure the woman had not connected with the skillet.

When he regained his senses Hank was standing over him laughing. The sight of Helen bounding out of the Bounder attacking a man with a skillet was just too much for him to keep a straight face.

"You shouldn't be laughing!" Helen said. "He has a gun in the back of his belt and was reaching for it when you walked up."

The man still laying on the ground said, "Lady, I was reaching for my wallet to show Mr. Moran my I.D. I am FBI Agent Crawford. Agent Emory sent me to meet with you."

Hank helped Agent Crawford to his feet. Helen apologized to Agent Crawford and said she was glad she didn't connect with the skillet.

"Lady! You're not the only one who's glad you missed," agent Crawford replied.

Hank asked if he was OK, if anything hurt.

"I'm OK, the only thing hurt is my pride," Crawford replied.

Agent Emory had brought Crawford up to speed on the investigation before he arrived at Timberfalls. The only thing he needed was to give Hank his cell phone number and to find out which trailer was Bixler's. Emory had emailed drivers license photos of both Bixler and Whitehead to Crawford. Crawford said he was all set and that he was going to get familiar with the tavern. Hank said he would probably see him there later. He was going to watch Bixler's trailer after dinner and would alert Crawford if there was any activity.

After dinner Helen went into the rear bath to transform herself into Henry. She removed all her makeup, removed her nail polish, and trimmed all her nails. She decided to braid her hair into a short ponytail. She had noticed a few of the other guests had a similar 'do. Hank had a sore knee awhile back and he had to wear an Ace Bandage knee wrap. She tightly wrapped it around her chest a few times and fastened it with safety pins. It did a good job of hiding her less than ample breasts. Earlier she had tried on one of her old plaid tops that looked mostly like a man's shirt and rolled up the sleeves. It looked like it would pass scrutiny.

She wore a dark t-shirt under the loose fitting shirt and denim shorts that weren't too tight. She finished with a pair of simple unisex leather hiking sandals.

When she showed Hank her outfit he said something was missing. He found an old Jack Daniels cap in his closet and stuck in on her head. She asked if she would pass for Henry and he gave her a thumbs up. All they needed now was dwindling daylight.

It was after eight o'clock and the sky was just starting to darken. Hank figured it was now or never and they headed down to the Heights campground for the party. The main purpose in going was to watch Calvin's trailer. Hank had checked in with Agent Crawford before they left and he assured them that Bixler and Whitehead were still in the trailer.

Hank and Henry, carrying two aluminum folding chairs, were welcomed by the group. Hank introduced Henry as his younger cousin from Kentucky. Henry was warmly greeted. Especially by Salvatore "Sally" Gallucci. Sally bragged that his surname meant "A lover of too many women," but in his case it was too many men. Needless to say Sally was immediately fascinated with Henry. He asked Hank if they were kissing cousins. Hank said they weren't because Henry has a partner back in the hills of Kentucky.

"You know what they say about those people from the Kentucky hills. I bet his partner is his cousin," Sally jokingly replied.

Henry joked, "Hell, when you're from Kentucky, and like us, you can't be too choosy. Anyways, it's not like we're going to reproduce."

This banter produced a roar of laughter from the group. Sally gave Henry a big hug and said, "Henry, just think of me as your big Italian cousin."

That produced more laughter. It appeared Helen's disguise was working and Hank and Helen were actually enjoying themselves at the party. There was even some entertainment when the Miller twins appeared in grass skirts and performed a hula dance to Hawiian music blaring from a boom box. Everyone was anticipating a wardrobe malfunction but were disappointed when thongs were discovered under the grass skirts.

Dewayne was at the party but was very quiet. He seemed to be watching Bixler's trailer as were Hank and Helen. About an hour had passed before Bixler's trailer door opened. Calvin and Franklin exited, acknowledged the gathering, and took off walking in the direction of the tavern. Hank noticed they were empty handed.

Hank stepped away from the gathering and called Agent Crawford. He told Crawford that the pair had exited the trailer and were heading towards the tavern empty handed. Crawford said he was in the tavern and would watch for them to arrive. Hank said he would join him shortly. He disconnected the call before Crawford had a chance to protest.

Hank took Helen aside and told her he was heading to the tavern. Helen said she was going back to the motor home before Sally got any more amorous. They bid goodnight to the rest of the party goers and left in separate directions.

Chapter 23

Wednesday, July 21st, 2010 – Timberfalls Resort

Calvin and Franklin entered the tavern and found two empty stools at the bar. The same bartender named Jake that Calvin had talked with in the morning was still on duty along with two others. Two scantily clad waiters were manning the tables.

Jake approached Calvin and said "Welcome back, what're ya'll havin?"

Calvin said, "Two of those cold drafts will do. By the way, this is my business partner, Frank, I told you about this morning."

"Oh yeah, you said you were planning to open a club down in Florida."

"That's right. Remember I told you I was very interested in installing an elevator like the one you have. I was wondering if you would let us take a look at it. I'd like to see its construction. We would like to take a ride on it if it's all right with you."

Jake replied, "I guess no harm can be done. It is designed to carry five hundred pounds. Ya'll just go in, close the gate and push the up or down button.

They finished their beers and told Jake they were going to look at the elevator. Jake told them to knock themselves out.

Hank and Agent Crawford were sitting at a table watching the brothers' conversation with the bartender. They were surprised to see the two brothers enter the elevator and disappear into the basement.

Directly below, Calvin and Franklin were examining the floor supports. Calvin said he would plant two charges. One on top of the two main center support columns tight against the heavy floor joists. Franklin noticed a propane

154

gas pipe was fastened to the side of one of the joists and smiled. He had also noticed a large propane tank outside next to the basement wall on their earlier approach to the tavern.

Franklin unlocked the exterior basement door for later access from the outside. The brothers then took the elevator back up to the bar level. After reclaiming their stools Jake asked what they thought. Calvin said it would work and said he was really excited to get back to Florida and begin construction.

The brothers ordered two more drafts and talked quietly among themselves. Franklin explained the plan to Calvin. Franklin would leave and go back to the trailer for the duffel bag. Calvin was to remain in the tavern and keep an eye on the bartenders. When he was ready to enter the tavern's basement he would call Calvin to check for the all clear. He would then enter and plant the charges. If Calvin saw any of the bartenders enter the elevator he should ring Franklin's phone once. And then once again for the all clear when the bartender reappeared.

Hank and Agent Crawford were at their table watching the two brothers when Dewayne walked in the door. Hank managed to grab him by the arm when he walked by their table and said very quietly, "Dewayne, we need to ask a big favor of you. This is Agent Crawford of the FBI and I am a private investigator working with him. It is very important when you talk with Calvin not to let him know who told you about his last name and his stepbrother. A lot of lives could depend on it."

Dewayne, giving Agent Crawford a mystified look, said, "Uh, OK, I guess I can do that."

Hank said, "Remember, Dewayne, a lot of your friends' lives could be at stake."

Dewayne just nodded and walked toward Calvin's spot at the bar.

As Dewayne was approaching, Franklin stood up to leave and gave Calvin a thumbs up saying he would call him later. Franklin walked past Hank's table and out the door. Crawford said he was going to follow him. Hank said he would keep an eye on things inside the tavern.

Hank observed as Calvin and Dewayne held a long conversation. It appeared they were on good terms and cementing their friendship. He saw with surprise that Calvin put his hand on Dewayne's knee. Dewayne put his hand on top of Calvin's.

Just then Calvin's cell phone vibrated in his pocket. Calvin answered the phone and held a brief conversation with the caller. He finished with, "Everything's just fine at this end," and disconnected. Calvin laid his cell phone on the bar.

When Helen left Hank to go back to the motor home she circled around and came back to the gathering of party goers. Most were getting ready to leave for the tavern. She singled out Salvatore and pulled him aside. Salvatore gave who he thought was Henry a big smile and said, "Hello, cousin!"

Helen said, "Sal, it's not what you think. I need to ask a big favor of you. I am working with the FBI tracking down a serial killer and need your help."

"Wow," he replied, "How can I help? I don't know anything about police work."

Helen replied, "All I need you to do is keep a lookout while I search that Denali fifth wheel down there. If you see the owner or his guest coming back knock three times really hard on the side of the trailer. And be very careful; they are dangerous people. Don't let them see you."

"If that's all you need, cousin, I can do that provided you let me buy you a drink at the tavern later."

Helen said, "You're on, Sal."

Helen approached the Denali and found that Calvin had left the door unlocked. She entered and began searching for the dynamite.

Franklin was walking back the trail to the campground when he sensed someone was following him. He quickly rounded a sharp bend and hid behind a large oak tree. He picked up a rock about the size of a softball that was next to the tree trunk and waited. As Agent Crawford approached he recognized him as one of the two men that were sitting in the tavern watching him and Calvin. They didn't know it but he was also watching them through the large mirror behind the bar.

He let Crawford pass then quickly sneaked behind him and smashed the rock into the side of Crawford's head just behind his right ear. The FBI agent fell without a whimper. Franklin quickly dragged him off the path and into the underbrush. He did a quick search and found the agent's wallet, cell phone and his .40 caliber Glock. The agent's ID was in his wallet. Franklin replaced the wallet and hid the Glock next to the tree trunk under some leaves. He smashed the cell phone against a rock and tossed it into the woods. Whispering, "Sleep tight, Agent Crawford. I'll be back," he was once again on his way.

Sal saw Franklin coming up the path and rapped three times on the trailer's side wall. He quickly ran around the other side of the neighboring trailer and walked towards Franklin. Salvatore tried to engage in conversation with Franklin to give Henry more time but Franklin would have none of it. He rudely said, "Excuse me," and brushed past.

Inside the Denali Helen heard the loud rapping and tried to find a place to hide. She didn't want to be seen coming out of the trailer. She remembered when she and Hank were looking at RVs that the beds in these trailers were hinged with storage underneath. She quickly scooted to the front of the trailer and lifted up the bed which had gas piston assists. The only things in the under the bed storage were a pile of blankets and a green duffel bag. She quickly crawled into the space and pulled the bed down. It came down with just a little tug. She supported it as she let it down so it wouldn't slam and make noise. She then made herself into as small a package as she could and covered herself up with the blankets. She reached over to feel the duffel bag and felt a bundle of cylindrical sticks. *Oh no*, she thought. *This must be the dynamite.* She quickly pulled her arm back under the blanket.

Helen was already sweating under the pile of blankets when someone entered the trailer. She heard the person rustle around a bit then enter the bedroom. She saw the light was then turned on through a small opening in the frame. She cringed and went totally rigid when the bed was lifted. She heard a man mumble something about what in hell all the blankets were for. Helen thought, *To cover me up asshole!* The bed was then let down and she heard the man sit on it. After a few moments he got up and she heard some more rustling around in some drawers. Shortly thereafter she heard the trailer door open and close and all was quiet. She reached for the duffel bag but it was gone. She laid there for a while to make sure the man wasn't coming back then was startled by three loud raps on the side of the trailer. *That must be Sal's all clear,* she thought.

Franklin was in a hurry and knew exactly what he wanted to do. He didn't remember why except maybe through force of habit that he brought his set of handcuffs along with him. He found the cuffs in his overnight bag and hooked them in his belt. He then went to the front of the trailer to the bedroom. He turned on the light and lifted up the bed. He saw the duffel bag and the large pile of blankets. He picked up the duffel bag and momentarily wondered why Calvin had so many blankets with him. After all it was July and he lived in Florida. He let the bed back down and sat on it. He checked the contents of the bag and everything was there including a large roll of duct tape. He found a pair of rolled up socks in one of Calvin's drawers and left. He wanted to make it back to the FBI agent before he woke up.

When Helen exited the trailer Sal was standing there and gave her a hug and asked if she was OK. Helen/Henry assured him that she was OK and told him about hiding under the bed. Sal said he was really worried about him. He was about to enter the trailer and make a rescue when the man reappeared from it. Sal asked if Henry found what he was looking for and Helen told Sal that she did but the man left with it. Sal said it was time to go to the tavern for that drink and Henry/Helen agreed.

On the way back to the tavern Franklin found that Agent Crawford was just starting to stir. Franklin sat him up against a tree and handcuffed his arms back around the trunk. He then stuffed Calvin's sock ball in the agent's mouth and sealed it in with three wraps of duct tape. Two extra wraps went around his eyes and the tree. With four wraps around the agent's ankles he was secured. He found the agent's Glock and put it in the duffel bag. He left wishing the agent a pleasant evening.

Franklin called Calvin as he approached the tavern. Calvin answered pretending to hold a short conversation with someone and gave the all clear. Franklin entered the basement and began his work.

When Dewayne approached Calvin his stepbrother was just getting up to leave. He heard the stepbrother say he would call him later, give a thumbs up, and walk past him to the door. Dewayne asked if he could have the stool and Calvin said he could.

"Calvin, why did your stepbrother have to leave?"Dewayne asked.

Calvin began to reply that his stepbrother had something to do when it dawned on him that Dewayne knew Franklin was his stepbrother.

"Dewayne, how did you know that was my stepbrother? I don't think I told you who my guest was."

"You didn't, Calvin. Someone else did."

"Come on, Dewayne. Who told you?"

"It was just some old guy I met on the trail. He wouldn't say who he was. He told me something else, too."

"What else did he tell you?"

"He said Bentley wasn't your real name. He said it was Bixler. Why did you lie and say it was Bentley?"

"Come on, Dewayne. I'll bet you half the guys up here don't use their correct names. There are always reasons you don't want certain people to know you were here at a place like this. I'm sure you know what I mean. Besides I don't think you ever told me your last name."

Dewayne thought a moment and said, "Heck, my last name is Heck."

Henry and Sal were walking down the trail to the tavern when they heard a moan off to the side of the wooded trail. Sal said, "Did you hear that? It sounded human." They stepped off the trail in the direction of the moan and saw a man handcuffed and duct taped to a tree. Sal cut the man free with a small pocket knife he always carried. Helen recognized him as Agent Crawford. Crawford said to check his right pocket for his keys. He said he left his handcuffs in his car but always carried a key on his key ring. Sal found the keys and released the agent. Crawford had trouble standing and leaned heavily on Sal and Henry. They made a decision to help Crawford back to the Bounder where he could lie down. The bruise on the side of his head looked nasty.

They made it back to the Bounder and Helen pulled out the sleeper sofa for Crawford to lie down. Helen asked if he knew who hit him.

Crawford said, I didn't see. I was following Whitehead up the trail and lost sight of him when he went around a sharp bend. When I went around the bend I was hit from behind.

Helen said, "Don't look at me; my skillet has been in the Bounder the whole time."

Crawford managed a halfhearted smile and reached for his wallet. He found it was still intact with nothing missing. He reached behind him and discovered his gun was gone. Crawford said, "Thank you for your help, Mrs. Moran. I have to get back to the tavern."

Helen said, "You're not going anywhere. I'm calling 911 for an ambulance. You probably have a concussion."

Crawford was about to protest when his eyes rolled to the top of his head and Sal helped him to gently settle onto the sofa bed. Helen immediately called 911.

When she got off the phone, Sal turned to her and said, "Henry, he called you Mrs. Moran!"

"I'm sorry, Sal. That's right. Hank is my husband and I am Mrs. Moran. My name is Helen, not Henry."

"Oh hell, just when I thought I found true love."

"You can't win them all," Helen replied, and gave Sal a hug and a kiss on the cheek.

Crawford moaned on the bed.

Hank was still at his table observing Calvin when he saw one of the bartenders approach the elevator and open the gate. He noticed that Calvin quickly picked up his phone and pushed a button. A moment later he laid his phone back down as the bartender disappeared into the basement. Five minutes later the bartender reappeared with three cases of beer. Calvin once again picked up his phone and pushed a button. A moment later he laid the phone down again.

He was sure Calvin's actions were a signal. He realized that Whitehead must be in the basement. Hank called Agent Crawford's number but received no answer. A few minutes later he saw Calvin once again pick up his phone. He was receiving a call. Hank saw Calvin mouth the word "OK," and a few other words and then hang up.

Franklin had set one charge up against the floor joist next to the gas pipe when his phone rang once. He picked up the duffel bag and just made it into a utility closet when he heard the elevator gate open. He found the short piece of half inch steel pipe in his bag and held it at the ready just in case someone was looking for a mop. He heard someone wrestling with some beer cases in the walk-in cooler, and then the elevator gate closed again. His phone rang once more and he went back to work.

A few minutes later he was done. Franklin set the latch for the basement door to lock behind him and he slipped out the door. He realized he'd forgotten the duffel bag but didn't catch the door in time and inadvertently grasped the doorknob. It was locked behind him. He called Calvin one more time, said he was finished, and told him about the bag. Calvin said not to worry and that he would take care of it.

Franklin walked quickly back the trail to where he had left the agent. When he found the tree the agent was cuffed to he saw that he was gone. Just pieces of duct tape scattered on the ground. He said, "Shit! What now? At least he's unarmed." He made it back inside the Denali and heard an ambulance coming through the campground with its siren blaring. Franklin followed the ambulance on foot up to the Heavens campground and watched the EMTs take the agent out of a motor home on a stretcher. He breathed a sigh of relief.

Calvin stood up from his bar stool and put his hand on Dewayne's shoulder. He said, "Dewayne, I have something very important to do. Meet me back in my trailer in a half an hour."

Calvin then walked briskly to the elevator, closed the gate, and descended into the basement. Hank sprang up and asked the bartender if there was another way into the basement. Jake the bartender said there was a set of stairs but they were being repaired and were unusable. They either had to use the elevator or the lower basement door. Hank told Jake to clear the Tavern because he was sure that there was a bomb just planted in the basement. Jake told another bartender to get on the PA system and have the place vacated. He told Hank to follow him as he pushed the button to have the elevator sent back up to the tavern level.

Calvin had just located one of the bundles of dynamite and put it in the duffel bag when he saw the elevator head back up. He was sure that whoever told Dewayne the information about him was right behind. He knew that older man looked familiar when he watched him in the bar mirror and was sure he was the retired detective his brother, Billy, told him about. In a panic he decided to forget about the other bundle. He unlocked the basement door and left.

Hank and Jake had just made it down to the basement as the outside basement door was closing. Jake ran towards the door and Hank yelled, "Forget about him. We have to find the bomb."

They searched around the floor and found nothing. Then Hank said, "Search the tops of these stone support columns."

A moment later Jake yelled that he had found something. Hank told him to keep looking while he checked it out. Hank quickly piled up two cases of beer, stepped up, and examined the bomb.

It looked like a simple bundle of dynamite with blasting caps. He looked at the bundle from the three visible sides and found no timer. He saw what looked like a radio wave receiver, a relay, and a capacitor that when activated would ignite the blasting caps. He shouted to Jake, "What's outside the door?"

Jake said it was just the driveway with the woods beyond. Hank told him to keep looking for another bomb. He gently removed the bundle of dynamite from atop the column and took it outside and forty yards into the woods. He managed to tear the duct tape that was wrapped around the bundle of four sticks and removed the blasting caps, thereby disarming it. All the time Hank was thinking, "Please, Calvin, don't push the button."

When Calvin entered his trailer Franklin was there waiting for him. "Good, I see you recovered the bag. Let me show you how the remote transmitter works then I'll be on my way."

Calvin found the remote in the duffel bag and handed it to Franklin. He didn't want Franklin to know there was also one of the bundles in the bag.

Franklin said it was really simple. There was just one toggle switch and one pushbutton. He explained to Calvin, "The toggle switch is a safety device. The pushbutton will not work unless the toggle switch is in the 'ON' position. This will prevent accidental activation of the bomb. Both bundles are set to receive the same radio frequency. The range of the transmitter is seventy-five yards so you will have to be about halfway to the tavern from here for it to work."

Calvin said he understood. Before Calvin could stop him, Franklin opened the duffel bag to replace the transmitter and saw the bundle of dynamite.

"What the hell is this, Calvin? What did you do?

"I can't go through with the bombing, Franklin. I changed my mind. While up here I found who I really am. I just cannot go through with it. I think I'm gay."

"I think you're fucking unbelievable! Where in hell is the other bundle?"

"I only had time to find the one bomb. There was someone right behind me coming down the elevator. I'm sure it was that detective Billy told us about. They had to have found the other bomb by now."

"You stupid sonovabitch! I thought we could pull this off without anyone knowing who helped you. Now I'm in shit just as deep as you. I'm out of here."

Dewayne was trotting up the drive when he saw Franklin leave Calvin's trailer and run towards the main parking lot. Dewayne knocked on the trailer door and heard Calvin answer, "Who is it?"

"Calvin, it's me, Dewayne, you said I should meet you here."

Calvin opened the door and let Dewayne in. Calvin opened the duffel bag and removed agent Crawford's Glock, pointed it at Dewayne and said, "Please, have a seat."

Chapter 24

Wednesday, July 21st, 2010 - Timberfalls Resort

Franklin was on his way out the driveway at
Timberfalls when a blue Crown Vic with tinted windows
and blue lights flashing passed him on the inbound side.
Agent Emory had trouble getting close to the tavern with
the huge crowd milling about the driveway. He had to
continually blow his horn as the crowd slowly parted to let
him through. Hank greeted Agent Emory when he exited
his vehicle.

"Hello, Chris. You got here fast."

"I was already on my way here when you called, Hank.
Where's the bomb?"

"I carried it about forty yards back in the woods. It's
OK, Chris, I disarmed it."

"Damn it, Hank, where's Agent Crawford? I tried to call
him, but he didn't answer."

Just then Helen appeared behind Hank. "Agent
Crawford is on his way to the hospital with a nasty head
bruise and possible concussion."

"Mrs. Moran, how did Crawford get injured?" Emory
asked.

"I don't know exactly. Sal and I found him handcuffed
to a tree and all duct taped up. He was barely conscious."

Hank said, "The last time I saw Agent Crawford he said
he was going to follow Whitehead when he left the tavern."

"I bet it was Whitehead who knocked out Crawford,"
Helen said. "He was on his way back to Bixler's trailer for
the dynamite."

"Mrs. Moran, how do you know the dynamite was in
Bixler's trailer?"

Helen glanced at Hank and Hank almost imperceptibly
shook his head no. She knew Hank meant not to divulge
the truth. She said, "It's a long story, Agent Emory. We still
have to find out if Bixler is up to more shenanigans."

"Chris, how many sticks of dynamite were stolen from the construction firm down in Florida?" Hank asked.

"ATF Agent Haas said the owner was sure that eight sticks were missing."

"There were only four sticks in the bomb I found. Bixler and Whitehead must still have the rest."

"Whitehead is gone," Helen said. "I saw him come out of Bixler's trailer and run towards the main parking lot. He wasn't carrying the green duffel bag that held the dynamite. The way he was moving he's probably halfway to Florida by now. After Whitehead left I saw Dewayne go into Bixler's trailer."

Emory said, "OK. The Baileyton police should be here any minute. I also called the Bristol bomb squad and they are on their way. They will dispose of the bomb Hank found and make a more thorough search of the tavern. Now, where is Bixler's trailer?"

Dewayne's eyes got as big as moon pies when he saw the gun pointed at him and said, "Calvin, what are you doing? Why are you pointing a gun at me?"

"Dewayne, just sit down and listen. I have something very important to tell you before I do what I have to do. I came up here to Timberfalls for only one reason. That reason was to plant some bombs where they would do the most damage and kill as many people as possible. What I wasn't counting on was meeting someone like you. I have grown very fond of you, Dewayne, and I realized I truly am one of the people that I came up here to destroy."

"My brother, the Reverend Billy Brantley, kept preaching to me that homosexuals were an abomination in God's eyes and should be killed. It said so in the book of Leviticus. The more he preached the more I believed him. Especially when he told me he killed one of them down in Gulf Breeze three weeks ago. He said he was only doing what God commanded and that God would smile upon him."

"Calvin, your brother is crazy," Dewayne said. "All that preaching has gone to his head. All those Old Testament books are just Jewish folk tales. Calvin, we were born this way. There is something different in our genetic structure.

We have no choice as to who we are. If your brother thinks that homosexuality is an imperfection, then wouldn't that make his God imperfect? And why would he want man to destroy these so-called abominations, these 'mistakes' He made? To cover His ass? Calvin it is all bullshit."

"Dewayne what you say may be true, but it's too late for me. I also killed two gay men. One was in Chattanooga and it pains me greatly to tell you that the other one was your friend, Donny Fleet, in Biloxi."

Just then there was banging on the trailer door and they heard, "FBI. Open the door and come out with your hands up."

Calvin yelled back, "Back away from the trailer. I have a gun and a bomb and will use them. I have Dewayne Heck in here with me. I will be sending him out in a minute with instructions for you."

Outside the trailer Agent Emory began warning everyone to back off away from the trailer. "Hank, the Baileyton police are arriving. Have them keep at least a hundred yard perimeter around Bixler's trailer."

Hank, Helen, and Sal were already urging the gathering onlookers to back off. When they mentioned the word bomb there was an immediate voluntary reaction to vacate the premises.

Dewayne just sat dumbfounded in the chair with tears in his eyes. He couldn't think of a single thing to say. He just sat and stared at Calvin with a pitying look. Staring at the man who killed his best friend in Biloxi. The same man he had also recently developed fond feelings for.

Calvin was writing on a notepad while he held the gun on Dewayne. When he finished writing he folded the note and handed it to Dewayne.

"Dewayne, give this note to the FBI agent when I let you go. Tell them outside they have fifteen minutes to remove any personal belongings from the trailers next to mine. I will fire my gun one time when time is up to warn them to clear the area. Tell them not to try anything cute or they will go up with me. Now get out of here."

Dewayne exited the trailer and found Agent Emory. He handed Emory the folded note and told him of Calvin's instructions. Emory yelled to the crowd behind him, "If any of you have anything in the trailers around that Denali fifth wheel you have less than fifteen minutes to get it out. If you hear a gunshot get the hell out fast."

A half dozen men immediately ran towards their rigs. A few hurriedly disconnected the power lines to their class C motor homes and pulled out dragging the sewer and water lines behind them. Others rescued a few things from their trailers and hopped into their tow vehicles and wheeled to the back of the campground.

They were all through and at a safe distance when they heard the gunshot.

Calvin saw that the fifteen minute mark was approaching. He picked up his cell phone and called his stepbrother, the Reverend Billy Brantley. Brantley had caller ID.

"Calvin, I told you to call only if there was an emergency."

"You can consider this an emergency if you want, Billy. I found I couldn't go through with the plan. I told them everything about what we had planned and about the people we murdered. I believe you are wrong in all of your preaching. These are good, decent people up here. They are not so-called abominations. I found out while I was up here that I am one of them."

Calvin fired the Glock up through the ceiling of the trailer.

"Calvin, what was that? Calvin are you there?"

"I'm still here, Billy. That was just a warning for everyone to clear the area."

"Calvin, what do you mean clear the area? What are you going to do?"

Calvin replied, "I'm sure you'll see it on Fox News, Billy."

Calvin pushed the toggle switch to arm the pushbutton. He had placed the dynamite directly under the sofa he was sitting on. He softly said, "An eye for an eye. Goodbye, Dewayne" and depressed the button.

They all heard the warning shot. Everyone who wanted to save their belongings had done so in plenty of time. All were on safe ground a hundred yards from the Denali.

They saw the walls expand and the roof begin to lift off before they heard the sound. When the boom like a loud peal of thunder reached them a quarter of a second later they noticed the body airborne with parts of the trailer roof. The body and large pieces of the roof landed on top of a neighboring trailer. For a brief time debris settled to the earth, then all was quiet.

Chapter 25

Agent Chris Emory opened the note that had been handed to him by Dewayne Heck and started to read. Hank could tell by the grin on his face that it was something good. "Hank, this is a full written confession by Bixler to the murders in Biloxi and Chattanooga. Not only that, he says the good Reverend Billy Brantley committed the one in Gulf Breeze Florida. He said that Whitehead had no involvement in any of the murders."

Hank said, "Whitehead might not have been involved in the murders, but he sure as hell was involved in the making and planting of the bombs. And add to that assaulting a federal agent. Even if it is mostly circumstantial evidence there should be enough to convict him."

"Why would someone like Whitehead even get involved in the scheme?" agent Emory asked. "He had a good job and position and no prior trouble with the law."

Hank replied, "Maybe he was just as nuts as his brothers and it took a while to surface. Or it could be his job. He probably gets off on the adrenalin rush working on the bomb squad. Maybe things got too quiet for him in Jacksonville and he needed the excitement. After all it is a known fact that firemen have set fires for the same reason."

A multistate order to apprehend went out for Brantley and Whitehead. The Baileyton police checked the Cedar Springs Campground and found Brantley's Montana fifth wheel, but the reverend and his truck were gone. They figured he left the trailer behind as it would slow his getaway. A search of Brantley's trailer produced a .38 special revolver.

Six o'clock the next morning Franklin pulled into his driveway in Jacksonville, entered his house, and turned on Fox News. They were airing a story about an explosion in a gay men's resort in Northeastern Tennessee. He thought, *The dumb shit blew himself up!*

Two FBI agents from the Jacksonville field office were waiting down the block when Franklin arrived home. They drove up to Franklin's house, parked behind his SUV, and knocked on the door. Upon seeing their presented I.D. Franklin invited them in.

The story was still playing on Fox News when they handcuffed him and led him out the door.

Brantley drove all night. He stopped to take a brief nap at the Information Center on Interstate 75 on the Georgia-Florida border. He figured the police would be waiting for him if he went to his house. He made it to the Bank of America office in Ocala by ten-thirty in the morning.

He withdrew fivethousand in cash from the eight-thousand he had remaining in that account.

His next stop was at the Car Max superstore in Orlando where they offered him twenty-two-thousand for his F-250 truck. He said they were trying to rob him, but he would take the deal if a check was immediately available. He turned over the title, and with check in hand, rode a cab to the nearby Bank of America to cash the check.

After verifying his account and the Car Max account the assistant bank manager OK'd the transaction. The waiting cab then dropped him off at the small plane charter terminal of the Orlando International Airport. He had called ahead and a single engine Cessna Skylane was waiting for him for the hop to Miami International.

Agents from the FBI field offices, with the help of the local police departments, were watching for his truck at all entrances to Orlando and Miami International airports, Brantley was already inside Miami International at an American Airlines gate boarding the 4:55 flight to Guayaquil, Ecuador.

He had paid cash for the ticket and used his second ID. One year ago on a business trip to Orlando he met with a gentleman who provided him with the identity of Claude Benson. At the time he did this on a whim for no more of a reason than fun.

The idea came to him when he learned about his stepbrother Calvin's dual personality disorder. The individual who had provided him with a Social Security number and Florida driver's license under the Benson name charged twelve hundred dollars for his services. The real Claude Benson died forty years ago at nine years of age.

As part of the same business trip to Orlando his flight to Belize was the topping on the cake. There he set up accounts in the name of an offshore business company under the name of "Southland Evangelical Ministries." He was listed as the sole director. All his funds were transferred into the Belize account except for the eight grand in Bank of America. The OBC gave him absolute secrecy and protection.

Unknowingly at the time he had prepared well for the present turn of events. He was sure now that God had been guiding him the whole time. *After all*, he thought, *God works in mysterious ways.*

With a passport under the Benson name he was all set. He had acquired the passport for five hundred dollars a week ago in Chattanooga. The gentleman who did the work was recommended by his peer in Orlando.

Brantley had spent missionary time in Ecuador shortly after his graduation from seminary school. During the two years he spent there he grew to like the country and the people. He estimated that with the twenty-three-thousand he had in cash he could get lost in one of the small mountain towns and survive for the better part of a year. He figured that after a year it would be safe to access his account in Belize and begin living the good life in Guayaquil. If not, he had been poor in the past and he knew he could survive.

Epilogue

Activities rapidly returned to normal at Timberfalls. The main topic of discussion at the tavern for the next few weeks was the attempted terrorist bombing. The eyewitnesses to the explosion of the terrorist's trailer delighted in telling how they saw his body sail through the air and land atop another trailer thirty feet away.

Hank was presented a lifetime honorary membership in the Timberfalls Resort.
The Mr. Timberfalls contest was held right on time. Helen was asked to be an honorary judge for the contest but she cordially recused herself. She said she could not be impartial with Salvatore Gallucci in the contest. Salvatore won the event dressed in a pink, sequined Speedo, but the Morans did not attend the contest as they had left the resort the Friday before to return to Kenner.

Hank had Helen promise that under no circumstances would she hide under any more beds.

Bill Anspach saw CNN coverage of the blast at the gay resort and immediately called Hank for all the details. The story appeared in Bill's travel column in the Sunday *Indianapolis Star*.

A week after the Morans returned to Kenner, Helen received a large envelope in the mail postmarked Baileyton, Tennessee. Inside was an eight by ten color photo of Salvatore in his winning pose for the Mr. Timberfalls contest. It was signed:

To Henry
From your big Italian cousin.
Sal

173

Dewayne Heck founded a gay and lesbian advocacy group in Biloxi under the auspices of a main group in Jackson, Mississippi. The group's mission statement included the education of the public on the gay and lesbian lifestyle and fundraising for scientific research to discover the homosexuality gene.

Charges of conspiring to commit an act of terrorism and assaulting a federal officer were formally brought against Franklin Whitehead.

Whitehead told the story that he suspected that his stepbrother had indeed stolen the dynamite from the construction firm in Florida. He traveled to Timberfalls to try to talk Calvin out of doing something foolish. Calvin had denied stealing the dynamite and said he was at Timberfalls because he realized he was gay and then found a friend in Dewayne Heck.

Franklin said he believed him and returned to Jacksonville. However, the FBI found Whitehead's fingerprints on the knob of the tavern basement door. In addition he was seen walking toward the tavern carrying the green duffel bag. The duffel bag was found mostly intact in the rubble of Bixler's trailer with some remaining blasting caps and part of a remote detonator.

Hank and Helen Moran were scheduled to be witnesses at the ensuing trial.

The FBI found no trace of Reverend Brantley. Agent Emory said it was as if he just vaporized. They knew he inherited a large sum of money but could find only one account in his name at the Bank of America. That account only had three-thousand dollars on deposit. His truck was located at Car Max in Orlando and they knew he had cashed the $22,000 check at a Bank of America but that was where the trail ended.

The cab driver who picked up the fare at Car Max had no recollection of the man he picked up. The hundred dollar tip he received to turn the meter off after the stop at the bank helped greatly to cloud his memory.

Two weeks later Agent Emory received a call from Hank inquiring about the status of the Reverend Brantley search.

Chris updated Hank and admitted they had reached a dead end. However they were able to match the ballistics of the .38 revolver found in Brantley's trailer to the murder in Gulf Breeze.

Hank said, "Chris, what was the estimate of his net worth?"

"We figure he should have about $1.3 million stashed somewhere. Possibly in an offshore account. He most likely has skipped the country."

"Chris, in my experience, a fugitive more often than not runs to some place he is familiar with. Has anyone checked into his history? It is quite common for recent seminary grads to volunteer for missionary work before they settle down to a steady ministry. It looks awfully good on their resumes. I would check the churches where he held positions to see if they still have his resume on file."

"Hank, you might have hit on something there. If we can nail down a country we can flood the place with his picture. A lead just might materialize."

"Now you're cookin, Chris"

After he ended the call Helen asked who Hank had been talking to. He said it was agent Emory and added, "Some people you just have to lead around by the nose."

About the Author

L.D. Knorr was born and raised on a dairy farm in Berks County Pennsylvania and now resides in rural Alabama. His profession as a mechanical engineer required his relocation from Pennsylvania to Mississippi, Texas, and Alabama. He honed his writing skills on engineering-related technical papers and reports. Now retired, he is focusing his attention on fiction.

He travels in his RV trailer with his wife Emily to visit family in Pennsylvania and Mississippi. They have been married forty-eight years and were blessed with three fantastic and creative children.

The idea for this first novel arose while discussing with a co-worker and part-time preacher the root cause of homosexuality. The ongoing debate centered on whether the gay lifestyle was chosen by the individual or was due to genetics.

www.ingramcontent.com/pod-product-compliance
Lightning Source LLC
Chambersburg PA
CBHW020614250626
47154CB00004B/1500